Meg Roberts—She's never stopped loving her daughter's father, even though she hasn't seen him in almost seven years. Even though she believes that the handsome ex-KGB agent seduced her for political reasons…and left her pregnant. Now, six-year-old Anna is the most important thing in Meg's life—and Meg's greatest fear is that Kon plans to take their daughter away.

Anna Roberts—Her mother said that Anna's daddy could never come to see her because he lived far away, in Russia. But he's *here* and he looks just like the handsome Nutcracker Prince in Anna's favorite book. More than anything, Anna wants her daddy to live with them—wants them to be a real family.

Konstantin Rudenko—The former high-ranking KGB agent has defected to the United States— for the love of a woman and a child he's never met. His daughter, Anna. His *Anochka*. He's been in hiding and he now has a new name and a new identity. But he's still the same man who fell in love with a young schoolteacher visiting Russia seven years before. The woman he called Meggie.

Dear Reader,

When I was a little girl, the Christmas season was always
my favorite time of the year—and it remains so to this
day! The family parties where Santa appeared, the velvet
dresses and ribbons, the aroma of gingerbread baking, the
evenings at the ballet watching *The Nutcracker* performed
to Tchaikovsky's music—I loved it all. Like Clara, the
young girl in *The Nutcracker* story, I will never forget the
Sugarplum Fairy or the Nutcracker Prince.

When I was seven, my mother gave me a child's recording
of *The Nutcracker* ballet with words set to the music. I
played it for years. Now that I'm a mother, my children
play it, and my daughter intends to play it for *her* children.
There's something magical about that story, and the music.

I recently found myself fantasizing about the Nutcracker
Prince. I wondered what he'd be like if he really came to life.
Naturally he'd be Russian.... And I could see an adorable
little girl who yearned for a father's hugs and kisses.

But I didn't have a story yet. Not until one day when my
daughter came rushing into the house to tell me about her
favorite teacher's experiences in the former Soviet Union.
"Mom, did you know that when Jackie was teaching over
there she was assigned her own KGB agent? Don't you think
that would make the most fabulous Harlequin Romance?"

Well, I'll let you, the reader, find out exactly what I thought!

To my darling daughter, Dominique, and our dear friend
Jackie, I dedicate this book, with all my love and gratitude.

Merry Christmas, and happy reading!

Sincerely,

Rebecca Winters

THE NUTCRACKER PRINCE
Rebecca Winters

Harlequin Books

TORONTO • NEW YORK • LONDON
AMSTERDAM • PARIS • SYDNEY • HAMBURG
STOCKHOLM • ATHENS • TOKYO • MILAN
MADRID • WARSAW • BUDAPEST • AUCKLAND

ISBN 0-373-03340-0

THE NUTCRACKER PRINCE

Copyright © 1994 by Rebecca Winters.

CHAPTER ONE

"SHH, ANNA, HONEY. Remember, we can only sing to the music at home, not during the ballet." Meg Roberts quietly admonished her six-year-old daughter, who was sitting on her lap and blithely singing the words to the "Waltz of the Flowers" a little off-key.

Even though the Saturday matinee performance of the St. Louis ballet company's *Nutcracker* catered to families with younger children, Meg noticed a good number of adults in the audience, as well.

"I'm sorry, Mommy. When will the prince come out?" Anna whispered so loudly it drew a quelling look from an older woman seated in front of them.

Before Meg could caution her again, Anna put a finger to her own lips and flashed her mother a mischievous smile—a smile that never failed to swell Meg's heart with love and pride. Anna's exuberant personality shone through her sparkling eyes, which fastened in rapt attention on the dancers once more.

In the near darkness Meg studied her daughter. Anna's cheeks were flushed with the excitement of attending her first ballet. Though Christmas was only eight days away, Anna had talked of nothing but this day for more than a month; even now, she hugged the picture book of the *Nutcracker* to the bodice of the red velvet dress Meg had made for her.

The well-worn treasure brought from Russia went everywhere her daughter did. With its Russian printing Anna couldn't read the words, but it was the illustrations that captured her heart—particularly the ones of handsome Prince Marzipan fighting the Mouse King. From the very first instant she'd caught sight of his tall, uniformed physique, Anna had remarked on the dark hair and blue eyes similar to her own. Even more poignant, from Meg's point of view, was the fact that her daughter had endowed Prince Marzipan with all the qualities she attributed to the father she'd never seen or known.

The fact that the Prince did bear a striking resemblance to Anna's father made it impossible for Meg to put her own bittersweet memories away, especially since he'd given Meg the book in the first place. It was a constant reminder of the man who, with practiced ease, had made love to a foolish, vulnerable, starry-eyed Meg—the man who'd left her pregnant. But even without it, there was no forgetting Konstantin Rudenko. Not when Anna was the very image of him.

With each passing day Meg grew more troubled as she identified yet another similarity in their coloring and features. Every day she was beset by disturbing flashes of recall that refused to die. Certain facial expressions, the way Anna's head swiveled around when she heard something that interested her, all would trigger long-suppressed memories followed by waves of shame and humiliation. Especially now that Meg knew she'd been set up, lied to, used....

"Look, Mommy!"

The Russian cossack dancers came out to perform their gymnastic feats, and once again Anna forgot where she was and broke into more off-key singing about balalaikas and clicking feet.

"Quiet!" the older woman snapped over her shoulder, and this time several other people turned around, as well.

Mortified, Meg hugged her daughter tighter. "You mustn't talk or sing," she whispered into Anna's short dark curls. "You're disturbing other people. If you make another sound, we'll have to leave."

"No, Mommy," she begged with tears in her eyes. "I haven't seen the prince yet. I promise to be good."

"You always say that, and then you forget."

"I won't forget," Anna asserted so earnestly Meg had to smile. Still, she knew it would be a sheer impossibility for her daughter to remain quiet throughout the rest of the performance.

"You'll have to stay on my lap."

"I will." She wrapped her arms around Meg's neck and gave her a kiss on the cheek before settling down. For a little while, Anna's model behavior lulled Meg into a false sense of security, and they both watched spellbound as the delightful story unfolded.

Then the symphony's brass section announced the arrival of the toy soldiers. Without warning, Anna slid off Meg's lap. "There's Prince Marzipan, Mommy. See?" she cried in ecstasy, pointing to the male dancer who led the march. Her absorption with the Prince made her oblivious to everything else around her, but

Meg hadn't missed the furious glare of the woman in front of them.

Luckily by now, other enchanted children throughout the audience had gotten to their feet and were contributing to the heightened noise. Their cheers and clapping made Anna's outburst seem less noticeable. From the glow in her eyes, Meg knew what this moment meant to her daughter, who stood entranced until the Prince leapt offstage after defeating the Mouse King.

The second he disappeared Anna whirled around and climbed onto Meg's lap again. "Mommy," she said in a loud whisper, "I have to *you know what.*"

Meg shouldn't have been surprised. The excitement had been too much, and she knew Anna wouldn't be able to wait until the performance was over. "All right. Don't forget your book." Throwing their coats over one arm, she reached for Anna's hand with the other and they made their way past several people to the center aisle.

"Slow down, honey," Meg cautioned, struggling to keep up with Anna who practically ran to the ladies' lounge off the nearly empty foyer. She was still chattering about the Prince when they emerged a few minutes later.

"Can I go see him when it's over, Mommy?" Anna blurted while they stood in the short lineup at the drinking fountain before going back into the concert hall.

"I don't think that's allowed."

"Mrs. Beezley said I could."

"We'll see," Meg murmured, wishing Anna's first-grade teacher hadn't put the idea in her head. Mrs. Beezley's opinions often carried more weight than Meg's.

"Our precocious daughter appears to be enjoying herself," Meg heard a male voice say from behind her. She assumed the man must be talking to his wife and didn't give it further thought as she waited for Anna to finish drinking from the fountain.

"Do you remember that lowly woodcutter's cottage outside St. Petersburg, *mayah labof?*"

Meg let out a gasp and the world came to a sudden standstill.

Konstantin. No. It couldn't be.

But his question, whispered with that quiet, unmistakable sensuality she remembered so well, spoke to the very depths of her soul. She hadn't imagined his voice.

Her body broke out in a cold sweat and she felt herself swaying. She closed her eyes in shock.

He was supposed to be living on the other side of the world, leading a life she would never want or be able to comprehend. Yet her heart beating frantically in her chest told her something vastly different.

He wasn't in St. Petersburg. He was *here*, in *this* theater, and he had just called her *my darling*. If Meg turned around, she'd be able to touch him.

Dear God.

But even as she recognized the reality of his presence, her body trembled in anger and panic. She was furious with herself for the weakness that brought the memories flooding back. The still-sensual memories of his lovemaking seven years ago—when she'd only been part of a night's work for him.

Her intellectual side had always known he was the enemy, but there was a time she'd been so in love with him her heart had refused to listen or care, had most of all refused to believe.

He knew about Anna.

The knowledge shouldn't have shaken her like this. Of course he knew about Anna. He knew things about people no human being had a right to know, because that was his business. His *only* business.

Which meant he'd been following them, waiting for the perfect moment to seize his property, to seize his daughter....

What better spot than someplace public, where he knew Meg couldn't or wouldn't make a scene because it would alarm Anna? Sick with fear, Meg felt her heart race out of control.

With startling clarity she remembered those terrifying hours she'd spent in the dark—alone—on the dank floor of a Moscow jail, her guards devoid of compassion or pity.

"Meg?" His voice interrupted her thoughts. She didn't know how much time had passed—only seconds, she supposed, but that was long enough to relive the years of heartache. She did not turn around as he began to speak.

"I don't know what you've told her about her father, but now that I'm here, we'll tell her the truth together. Forget any ideas of running away from me, or I will most assuredly cause a scene. Since I know how much you would hate to upset Anna, I expect your full cooperation.''

His English was as perfect as ever, formal, precise. The training he'd received in the KGB left nothing to chance. Anyone listening would assume he was from the United States, perhaps the East Coast.

A moan escaped her lips, and the sound caught Anna's attention. She gave up her place at the fountain for the next child. ''Mommy? What's wrong?'' Apprehension gripped Meg so tightly she couldn't move or breathe; it prevented her from doing any of a dozen things her survival instincts screamed for her to do. No trap ever devised worked as well as the threat to one's own flesh and blood. ''N-nothing, honey. Let's hurry back inside.''

She grabbed Anna's hand and almost dragged her toward the doors of the concert hall. Meg knew she didn't have a prayer of eluding *him*, but she refused to remain there like a paralyzed animal while he gloated over another easy victory.

''Mommy, you're hurrying too fast,'' Anna complained, but Meg, whose fear escalated with every passing second, increased her speed.

It didn't matter that there had been drastic changes in Russia since detente. He might no longer be KGB, but he could still be working for the present powers in a classified capacity. Secret police still existed in the former USSR.

As far as she was concerned, he was a dangerous man she'd never wanted to see again—a man who could pass himself off as an American, with no one the wiser—a man who now walked within whispering distance of them and had obviously been monitoring the events of her life for years.

He was a man who would stop at nothing to achieve his objective. And she had an idea his objective now was Anna.

But this time there was one difference. She was no longer that naïve twenty-three-year-old who had credited him with a set of values similar to her own. Time and experience had worked their damage, and that vulnerable young creature no longer existed. All that remained of their long-ago nights of passion was Meg's bitterness—and her daughter.

If she and Anna could make it inside before he caught up with them, she could buy a little time to work out what to do. By now she was half-pulling, half-carrying Anna, her own heart pumping hard and fast.

"Meg? Anna?"

At the sound of their names being called, Anna yanked free of her mother and turned around. "Who are you?" she asked, her face bright with curiosity.

Defeated by his cunning, Meg was forced to come to a stop and face the man she'd once, briefly, loved. The man who had fathered Anna. She didn't want to look at him, didn't want to acknowledge him. But Anna was watching them with avid interest, and Meg was afraid to upset her or force his hand too soon.

When she finally dared a glimpse, the intense blue of his heavily lashed eyes almost made her reel. He'd always been the most attractive man she'd ever known, yet he looked different, somehow, from the way she remembered him.

The first time she'd met him, his brown-black hair had brushed the collar of his drab gray suit and trench coat, typical KGB garb. Now he wore his hair shorter and dressed like a successful American businessman in a navy suit and pale blue shirt that enhanced his six-foot height and lean, muscled frame. But the difference she perceived was subtler than that.

Unlike the married middle-aged men at the European-auto dealership where she worked as a secretary/cashier, he'd grown even handsomer, if that was possible, over the past seven years. In his late thirties now, he possessed a virile appeal that her body recognized and responded to without any volition on her part.

"I'm someone who loves you and your mommy very much," he said in answer to his daughter. Anna resembled him in so many attractive ways, Meg was afraid she'd see the similarities right off.

"You do?" Anna sounded amazed and, worse, intrigued.

Meg's eyes closed in growing fury. He meant business. Damn him for his matchless ability to charm his victims. As always, he resorted to ways that had nothing to do with brute force.

With an overwhelming sense of helplessness she waited to hear his response, part of her still denying he had sprung out of nowhere like one of those disturbing dreams that haunts you for years afterward.

"What's your name?" Anna asked softly.

"Konstantin Rudenko."

"K-Konsta . . . What did you say?"

He chuckled. "Your mommy calls me Kon."

The audacity, the cruel, calculating arrogance of the man, filled Meg with rage.

"It's Russian, like yours."

"You mean I have a Russian name, too?"

"That's right." He pronounced it with his native accent, his voice tender. Then his eyes sought Meg's as if to say, "You've never forgotten me."

"No!" Meg cried out against this threat to her fragile emotions and hard-won independence, but it was too late. In a quick, protective move she placed both hands on her daughter's shoulders.

Anna's young, inquiring mind seized upon the information she'd just learned and carefully imitated his pronunciation of her name. She tried to pull away from her mother. "My mommy told me my daddy lives in Russia, so he can't ever come to visit me," she said in a loud whisper, remembering too late that it was a secret between the two of them. Her mother had told her over and over that no one else must ever know.

"Anna!" Meg chastised her, but the effort was fruitless.

"Well, your mommy is wrong, Anochka," he asserted, using the diminutive of her name.

This time Anna wriggled loose from Meg's grip and moved closer to inspect him. "You look just like Prince Marzipan!"

Quick as lightning she peered over her shoulder at Meg, who was shaken by the stars in her daughter's eyes. "Mommy! He looks like the Prince!" And she immediately opened her book to the page whose edges were worn from constant use. "See?" She pointed out the similarities to him.

In a lithe move he got down on his haunches, making it easier for Anna to show him her proof. A satisfied smile lifted the corners of his mouth, and he fingered one of the curls bouncing over her forehead. "Did you know I gave your mommy this book when she left Russia after her first visit, more than twelve years ago?"

For the second time in a couple of minutes, Meg gasped out loud. Anna's eyes grew huge. "You did?"

"Yes. It's my favorite book, too. That's because we're father and daughter, and we think alike."

His eyes flashed Meg another meaningful glance. "Your mommy was sad because your grandfather died while she was on her trip. So when she went home, I put this book in her suitcase to comfort her because she had admired it. I hoped it would make her feel better and bring her back to Russia one day, because I cared for her even then."

Tears stung Meg's eyes. *Liar*, her heart cried. But she couldn't dispute the fact that this beautiful, overpriced book, which she'd admired at the House of Books in Moscow and couldn't afford, had ended up in her luggage. It was all thanks to the dark, attractive KGB agent, assigned to the foreign-student sector, who had hustled her from jail to the airport.

Meg, along with other seventeen-year-olds on her bus, had been detained because they'd given away blue jeans, T-shirts and other personal articles to friendly Russian teenagers. Unsuspecting, Meg had given her Guess? sunglasses to a young girl—and ended up in prison. She still shuddered when she thought of that nightmarish incident.

During her confinement, one of the guards told her the tour director had just learned that Meg's father had died back in the States. Because of Meg's unwise decision to break the law and consort with black marketers, he informed her, she might not be able to go home for the funeral, maybe not be able to go home at all.

He'd seemed inhuman to Meg, incapable of emotion. He'd left her alone to "think about" what she'd done, and Meg had collapsed on the floor in despair. For hours she'd sobbed out her grief for the loss of her mother a year earlier and now her beloved father. William Roberts was dead, thousands of miles away, and she would never see him again.

But before morning, Kon had come to get her, and she was escorted through hallways to a back door, where a car waited to take her to the airport. She never saw her traveling companions again, and returned to the United States in time to bury her father, the book her only memento.

After her cruel treatment at the hands of other agents under his command, Kon's authority and subsequent intervention had been the only reason she was allowed to return to the States without further repercussions. His gift, totally unsolicited, had caused her to rethink her opinion that all KGB agents were monsters.

Six years later, when she qualified for a new opportunity, arranged through the State Department, to travel to Russia as a cultural-exchange teacher, she looked forward to the experience. Meg had hoped to locate him and thank him in person for his kindness.

She'd seen him again, all right. Naively she'd believed that their meeting was accidental, never realizing that Kon had kept track of her back in the States. The knowledge was almost unbearable. It meant his feelings had never been real. And it meant that on her second trip to the USSR, after the invalid aunt she'd lived with and taken care of had passed away, Meg was targeted. She'd learned about this from the CIA on her return. Kon's every move had been calculated to make her fall in love with him, for reasons best known to the KGB. It had happened before, to equally naive, usually young American men and women—tourists, diplomatic employees and others. What had occurred between Meg and Kon was, as it turned out, not all that rare. Kon's "love" had been politically motivated; he'd been in control.

And now he'd come for Anna.

"Are you really my daddy?"

Anna's simple question broke the silence. The hope in her earnest young voice had Meg practically in tears. She realized they'd come to the moment of truth. Kon would show no mercy.

"Yes, I'm your daddy, and I can tell you're my little girl. We have the same blue eyes, the same dark brown hair, and the same straight noses." He tweaked hers gently, and Anna giggled. "But you smile just like your mommy. See?"

He whipped some pictures out of his suit-coat pocket. "That's your mommy and I eating ice cream and champagne. I'd just told her I loved her. Look at her mouth. It curves right there—'' he touched Anna's lower lip "—exactly like yours.''

Anna giggled again before putting the precious storybook on the floor so she could look at the black-and-white snapshot. For once in her life she was struck dumb. So was Meg, who could remember him touching her mouth like that. Then he'd kissed her until she'd never wanted him to stop....

At the time she'd been blissfully unaware that someone was taking pictures of them.

There had to be many more photographs where those came from. Meg had little doubt that a camera had recorded their days and nights together, and she felt a deep, searing pain that the most wonderful experience of her life—loving Kon—could have ended up in the KGB microfilm files.

"Mommy, look! This is a picture of you.''

"That's right,'' he murmured, "and here are some other photos of your beautiful mother and me in front of her hotel and at a nearby museum.''

Kon couldn't have come up with a more cunning plan to win over his daughter than this—offering her hungry eyes absolute proof of her parents' relationship.

On both of Meg's trips to Russia, picture-taking had been strictly forbidden, except for the shots taken at Red Square, the military pride of the nation. Which explained why she didn't have even one photograph of Kon to keep in remembrance.

"And here,'' he said when Anna had finished inspecting the others, "is a picture of your mommy and me at the airport. I begged her to stay in Russia and marry me, but she got on that plane, anyway." His voice sounded desolate, and Meg thought cynically that it was a mark of his consummate acting ability.

By now his arm had gone around Anna's tiny waist and she leaned against his chest without even realizing it. Watching her daughter, Meg felt her heart shatter into tiny pieces.

Anna raised troubled eyes to her mother. "Why did you do that, Mommy?" Tears threatened. "Why did you leave my daddy alone?"

Meg fought for a stabilizing breath, despising Kon for doing this to her. To them. "Because I couldn't have come back to America if I had stayed any longer, and I had responsibilities at home. Classes to teach, commitments to my students."

"You're a teacher?"

After a brief pause she said, "Not anymore, honey. But I was—once."

"Like Mrs. Beezley?" Anna sounded totally puzzled by her mother's admission.

"Yes. I taught high school." But having a baby on her own had forced her to grow up in a hurry, and when she realized the truth of what had gone on while she was in Russia, she gave up teaching Russian and wanted nothing more to do with the country, the language or her memories. Anna was too young to understand, so Meg had never told her about that aspect of her life.

Unfortunately Anna had found the *Nutcracker* book in a box in the storage room where Meg had hidden it. The little girl had fallen in love with it on sight and commandeered it for her own. Meg had never had the heart to take it away from her, but she'd never explained its origins, either.

"Is it true, Daddy?"

With that one question, Meg knew it was all over. Not only had Anna accepted Kon as her father without reservation, but now she was questioning Meg's veracity.

What an ironic fact of life that a mother could give her all to her child for six years, and then a man, whose only contribution had been biological, could come along and in a heartbeat win that child's unquestioned devotion and adoration.

"Yes, it's true. Your mother speaks excellent Russian, and when she wasn't teaching English to some Russian students, we spent every moment of her four months in St. Petersburg together."

Meg's breathing had grown shallow. "Anna...why don't you ask your father why he didn't come to America with me?" She knew her voice sounded brittle.

"But I did come," he countered with a swiftness that took her breath. "You see, in order to leave my country, I had many things to do first, many responsibilities. But I've always known about you, Anochka. I've always loved you, even when I was far away. Now I'm finally here, and I'm going to stay."

For as long as it took to win over Anna. Then he would disappear with her. Meg was sure of it. She wondered when this latent fatherhood instinct had taken over to bring him halfway around the world to claim his child.

"You can sleep in my room," Anna declared, tying up all the loose ends with the simple reasoning of an innocent child. She could have no comprehension of the scattered debris of their separate lives.

"I'd like that," he murmured softly. "That's why I've come—to live with you and your mommy. I want us to be a family. Can I ride home in your car? I didn't bring mine to the ballet."

"We have a red Toy-yoda. You can sit in the back with me and read me my book while Mommy drives us."

"We'll take turns reading. Do you like where you live?"

"Yes. But I wish we had a dog. The mean apartment man won't let us have one."

"Then you'll love Gandy and Thor." He bundled her in her winter coat while they chatted.

"Gandy and To—what?"

"Thor. They're my German shepherds, and I've told them all about you. They can't wait to get acquainted. And once they do, they'll play with you and be your friends forever." At his words, Anna squealed in delight.

Impotent rage welled up inside Meg. Nothing was beneath him, certainly not the wholesale bribery of his vulnerable daughter. Meg was close to screaming, but the *Nutcracker* had ended and people were pouring into the lobby. For Anna's sake, she had to keep tight control on her emotions until she could be alone with him out of her daughter's hearing.

Konstantin Rudenko was used to being an absolute, unquestioned authority in his own country, but there was no way she would allow him to strong-arm her here, in *her* home.

Meg marched over to her daughter and put a firm hand on her shoulder to separate her from her father. "Let's go, Anna."

But Anna wasn't listening. Her hands had reached out to explore the texture and hard coutours of Kon's face. For a traitorous moment Meg relived the sensation, the slight raspy feel of those cheeks against hers after she spent the night in his arms. Making love...

"Will you let me carry you to the car, Anochka? I've dreamed of holding my own little girl for a long, long time."

Anna, who up to this point hadn't liked any man who paid too much attention to Meg, was obviously mesmerized by his husky voice and the loving look in his eyes. She slid her arms around his neck and let him pick her up, her expression one of sublime joy.

"What does that *noska* word mean?"

"My little baby Anna. That's what the daddies in Russia call their darling daughters."

"I'm not a baby. You're funny, Daddy." She gave him his first kiss on the cheek.

"And you are adorable, just like your mother." He crushed her in his arms, as if he'd been waiting his whole life for this moment.

Meg looked away, pierced to her soul to see Anna's enchantment with a man who wasn't beyond manipulating a child's deepest and most tender emotions to get what he wanted.

She would never forgive him for this. *Never.*

CHAPTER TWO

"WHICH WAY to your car, *mayah labof?*" he asked, repeating the calculated endearment that still had the power to touch her emotionally, though she fought against it. "Anna and I are ready."

Meg was on the verge of shouting that since he'd followed them to the theater, he no doubt knew exactly where her car was parked. But when she saw how perfect father and daughter looked together, with Anna's arm placed trustingly around his neck, Meg's throat choked up and no words would come.

Anna had wanted her own daddy from the time she'd watched her best friend, Melanie, with *her* father. It always made Anna feel left out. Within the last few minutes, though, bonds had been forged that no power on earth could break.

Other people leaving the theater would see at once that they were father and daughter, and Meg noticed how several women's eyes lingered on Kon's striking features.

If anything, it was Meg's relationship to the dark-haired little girl in his arms people might question. Meg's shoulder-length ash-blond hair and gray eyes suggested a different ancestry altogether—yet another irony Meg was forced to swallow. She fastened her coat against the cold, wintry afternoon and headed for her car, parked on a side street around the corner.

She walked several paces from Kon so she wouldn't accidentally brush against him. She felt relieved when he got into the back seat of the car with Anna, keeping some space between them.

He might think he had the upper hand now, especially while Anna clung to him and bombarded him with questions. But once they were home, they'd be in Meg's territory. *She'd* set the rules. They'd have dinner immediately, she decided, and as soon as Anna had eaten, it would be her bedtime.

With her daughter asleep, Meg would be able to have it out with Kon and get rid of him before Anna awakened. As soon as possible, Meg would contact the attorney who had helped settle her father's and aunt's affairs: she would get a court order forcing Kon to stay away from her and Anna.

Since no marriage had taken place and he wasn't an American citizen, she wondered what rights he had where their daughter was concerned. Certainly when her attorney learned the truth of Kon's KGB background, he would do everything in his power to protect Anna from being alone with her father—not to mention being taken out of the country. How she wished her Uncle Lloyd was still alive. He'd worked in navel intelligence and could have counseled her on the best way to proceed.

Meg had no idea how high up in the KGB Kon had risen, but she couldn't imagine him renouncing a system that had dominated his entire life. Of course, political ideologies weren't something she and Kon had discussed when they were together. He'd always managed to find them a place where they could be alone because they were so hungry for each other, could never get enough of each other. Their conversation had been that of lovers.

Evidently when his tactics had failed to get her to marry him—which would have meant turning her back on her own country—he'd had to devise another scheme. He'd decided to come after Anna. But he'd waited until she was old enough to respond to his machinations and his charms.

Maybe he genuinely wanted a relationship with his daughter, but Meg also knew how much he loved his country, how deeply immersed he'd been in its ideology. Naturally he would want Anna to feel the same way, and that meant taking her back there with him.

"Where are my dogs, Daddy?"

"At the house I bought for you and your mother."

"Oh, Mommy!" Anna cried joyfully and clapped her hands. "Daddy has a *house* for us! Where is it, Daddy? Can we go see it now?"

"I think your mommy has other plans for tonight," he told her.

Meg bit her tongue in an effort to keep quiet. She almost ran into a van standing next to the driveway that led to the parking garage of her apartment complex. Kon had deliberately brought up subjects guaranteed to delight a little girl starving for a father's love and attention. If Meg fought with him in front of Anna, it would only alienate her daughter and cause more grief.

And there would be grief.

But by the time Anna awakened the next morning, she would discover her father permanently gone from their lives. Meg wouldn't rest until she had some kind of injunction placed against Kon. Back at the apartment, she would manufacture a reason to run to one of her neighbors so she could phone Ben Avery in private. She didn't care if she had to keep her attorney and a judge up all night!

The second Meg pulled in her parking space and turned off the engine, Anna scrambled from the car, too involved with Kon to be thinking about her mother. "Come on, Daddy. I want you to see my aquarum." She couldn't quite manage the *i*. "You can feed my fish if you want to."

"I'd like that, but first we have to help your mommy," Meg heard him say in a low voice before he shut the rear door and opened the driver's side. She shouldn't have been surprised by his solicitude. Nothing was done without a motive, and she suspected he wasn't about to let her out of his sight.

Avoiding his gaze, she got out of the car, pulled away from the hand that gripped her elbow and walked ahead of them on trembling legs. She headed blindly toward the door leading into the modern, three-story complex.

It would have done no good to reach for Anna, who still clutched her book in one hand and her father's hand in the other, impatiently waiting to show him her world.

"Melanie lives right here!" she exclaimed as they passed a door on their way down the second-floor hall. "Is she your friend?"

"Yes, my best friend. But sometimes we fight. You know—" Anna leaned toward him confidingly "—she says I don't have a daddy."

"Then you'll have to introduce us later and we'll prove to her she's wrong."

Anna skipped along beside her father, her face illuminated with joy by his words. "She says my mommy had a *luvver*." This was news to Meg, who could feel her world falling apart so fast she didn't know how to begin gathering up the pieces. "What's a luvver, Daddy?"

While Meg cringed, Kon slowed his pace and picked Anna up in his arms once more. "I'm going to tell you something very important. When a man and a woman love each other more than anyone else in the world, they get married and become lovers. That's why you were born, and we both love you more than our own lives."

"But you and my mommy didn't get married."

"That's because we lived in different countries, which complicated everything. But now that I'm here, we'll get married and live happily ever after."

Meg could hardly breathe.

"Can you get married tomorrow?"

Kon laughed low in his throat. "How about next week at my house? We'll need to help your mommy pack everything and move out of the apartment first."

Terrified of creating a scene that would traumatize Anna and arouse even more interest from her neighbors—many of whom were just coming home from Christmas shopping with packages in their arms and had already noticed Kon holding Anna—Meg practically ran down the hall to her apartment. She'd hung a large holly wreath tied with a red ribbon on her door, but hardly noticed it now.

She fumbled with the key, trying to get it in the lock, Kon's mesmerising power over Anna frightened and enraged her. He'd learned his seductive techniques through years of KGB training. He'd learned to consider human feelings expendable.

"Take me to my bedroom, Daddy. My aquarum's in there," Anna dictated her wishes, pointing the way as he carried her across the small, modestly furnished living room Meg had cleaned earlier that day. The unlit Christmas tree stood in the corner, a slightly lopsided Scotch pine, but Meg couldn't afford anything better. Still, the gold and silver balls among the tiny colored lights looked festive when Kon stopped long enough for Anna to flip the wall switch so he could see the effect.

Meg closed the front door, ignoring the triumphant glance he cast her. He'd made it this far without her interference. As soon as they disappeared down the hall, she unbuttoned her coat and threw it over a chair, realizing this might be the only time she'd be free to talk to her attorney.

Mrs. Rosen, the widow across the hall, was a retired musician. She could usually be found at home this time of the evening giving violin lessons. Anna was her youngest student and had made significant progress in the past year. But Anna's musical ability was the last thing on Meg's mind as she let herself out of the apartment, praying the older woman was in so she could use her phone and ask her to keep an eye on

Meg's door while she made the call. Just in case Kon had thoughts of an immediate escape. . . .

"Ms. Roberts?"

Meg jumped, surprised to be met in the hall by a man and woman dressed in casual sports clothes and parkas. They stood in front of her, blocking her path.

The van that had been parked next to the driveway flashed into her mind, and a feeling of inevitability swept over her. Naturally Kon wouldn't have made his move without accomplices. More KGB? Since detente, they were officially known as the MB, but Meg knew very well that despite the chaos in Russia, they could still be dangerous. It was possible some of their operatives continued to function in the U.S. for counterintelligence purposes.

As if reading her mind, they both pulled identification from their pockets.

CIA. Meg swayed on her feet, and the dark-haired, fortyish woman put a hand on her arm to steady her. "We know the appearance of Mr. Rudenko has come as a shock to you, Ms. Roberts. We'd like to talk to you about it. Inside."

Infuriated, Meg jerked her arm free. "Do you actually expect me to believe you're from the CIA?" she hissed. "I know how the MB works. Just like the KGB! You pass yourselves off as anything you like, and you'd double-cross, triple-cross your own families if necessary."

The man, who wore horn rims and looked around fifty, gave her a patronizing smile. "Please cooperate, Ms. Roberts. What we have to tell you should abate your fears,'' he said with an exaggerated sincerity that nauseated her.

Meg stiffened. "And of course if I refuse, you'll force me back into my apartment at gunpoint. But since you know I'd never do anything to upset my daughter, you're confident I'll do whatever you ask.'' She turned and reentered her apartment, the two agents close behind.

Just then a door down the short hallway opened and a grim-faced Kon appeared, checking up on her, no doubt, to make sure she was cooperating. Just like old times. Of course back then she'd thought it was because he couldn't stay away from her. In the background she could hear water running and assumed he had talked Anna into taking a bath to distract her.

Meg stared into those damnably blue eyes. "You make me sick,'' she snapped. "The whole bunch of you! And—'' she pointed at Kon ''—as far as I'm concerned, if you've forsaken your own country, you're a traitor to all! Now why don't you leave unsuspecting people and children alone? Go find some uninhabited part of the world where you can play absurd war games to your hearts' content. If you battle each other long enough, none of you will be left alive—thank God.''

With a nonchalance that stunned her, Kon loosened his tie and removed his jacket. Without taking his eyes off her he tossed it on top of her coat, drawing her unwilling attention to the play of hard muscle in his arms and shoulders. He behaved as if this was an everyday occurrence in his own home.

"Anna's bath will be through in a few minutes, and then she expects to come out and eat dinner with us. She'll be alarmed if she hears you shouting like a fishwife, instead of being cordial to Walt and Lacey Bowman from the auto dealership where you work. Is that what you want?" He pressed the advantage. "Or shall I tell her that you've had to go back to the office on an emergency? There's a vacant apartment down the hall and I have the key. It's entirely up to you where this conversation takes place."

"Mommy? Daddy?" Anna burst into the room unexpectedly, dressed in pajamas dotted with kangaroos, her curls bobbing. But when she saw the strangers, her smile faded, and to Meg's intense relief she ran past Kon straight to her mother. Meg picked her up and held her tightly in her arms. If she had her way, she'd never let go of Anna again.

"Honey?" She strived to keep her voice from shaking. "These are the Bowmans. They work in the sales department at Strong Motors every day after I come home from the office." She was improvising, because they'd left her no choice. "You've never met them before."

The older woman smiled. "That's right, Anna. But Walt and I have heard a lot about you."

"You're a mighty cute little girl," the man chimed in. "You look a lot like your mommy and daddy."

"Daddy looks like Prince Marzipan."

The woman nodded. "I heard you went to the *Nutcracker* today. It's my favorite ballet. Did you like it?"

"Yes. 'Specially the Prince!"

Kon's eyes actually seemed to moisten as he lovingly fastened his gaze on his daughter. Meg turned her head away, astounded once again by his incredible acting ability.

"We need to talk to your mommy for a minute," the man continued. "Is that all right with you?"

"Yes. Daddy and I can fix dinner. We're going to have macaroni. Daddy says they don't eat macaroni in Russia. It's a . . . an Amercan invenshun."

"That's right, Anochka." He chuckled in delight. "I can hardly wait to try it. Come with me." In the next breath Kon plucked his daughter from Meg's arms and carried her to the kitchen and out of earshot, leaving Meg alone with the two agents. She'd probably never know who they really were or who they worked for. It could be either government—or both.

The older woman ventured a smile. "Do you mind if we sit down?"

Meg's hands tightened into fists. "Yes, I mind. Say what you have to say and go."

She knew her voice sounded shrill, but she'd been suppressing all that pent-up fear and rage since Kon had first ambushed them in the theater foyer. Right now she was on the verge of hysteria; she was ready to scream the apartment complex down, Anna or no Anna.

Everyone remained standing. The man spoke first. "Mr. Rudenko defected from the Soviet Union more than five years ago, Ms. Roberts."

Meg shook her head and let out a caustic laugh. "He's KGB. They don't defect."

His brows lifted. "This one did."

"If such a thing happened, then it was mere pretense so he could kidnap Anna at some point and take her back to Russia with him!"

"No," the woman interjected. "He became an American citizen this October. After the secrets he exchanged for asylum, he can never go back."

"Why should I believe you?" Meg exploded, the adrenaline pumping through her body so furiously she couldn't stand still. "In the first place, our government no longer needs to make deals with Russian defectors to get information. Not since detente. Now I want you out of here. Out of Anna's and my life!"

"We do make deals when it's a top-ranking KGB official," the man persisted. "One, I might add, who belonged to an elite inner circle and could shed light on highly sensitive issues—give us valuable information about the kidnappings of American citizens, both civilian and military, within and outside the Soviet Union."

The other woman nodded. "He never approved of those tactics in the old regime, nor the cruelty to Russians and non-Russians alike. That's one of the reasons he defected."

Grudgingly, Meg had to admit they were right about one thing. If Kon hadn't intervened, she might still be in that Moscow jail.

"The information he provided has answered questions our government never dreamed would be cleared up," the woman went on. "In some cases, the facts Mr. Rudenko obtained have relieved the speculation and suffering of families who've never learned what became of their loved ones."

"Mr. Rudenko has done a great service to our country and caused a good deal of embarrassment to his own," the man asserted in a firm voice. "Do you remember that news item several years ago about the missing airforce pilot—the son of an elderly woman living in Nebraska? His plane had disappeared over Russia almost fifteen years ago."

Meg's thoughts flashed back to the heart-wrenching story, which had been the main topic of the media at the time. She could still hear the woman sobbing with relief as much as sorrow—relief because the Pentagon had finally received positive proof of her son's death. She remembered the woman saying that now she could die in peace.

"That was thanks to Mr. Rudenko, who was able to provide detailed information about the pilot's incarceration in Lublianka prison and his subsequent death."

Meg's eyes narrowed on the two of them. She simply couldn't trust anything to do with Kon, who never made a move without a motive. She'd discovered, to her cost, that all his apparently generous actions— such as purchasing that book on the *Nutcracker* and putting it in her luggage—had a hidden purpose.

"Even if what you tell me is true," she said, "it changes nothing. There's something strange about a man who would defect as far back as five years ago, then wait until today to show up and declare that he wants a relationship with his daughter."

Her face twisted in pain. "As far as I'm concerned," she continued, her voice rising, "it's a lie, and you're part of it! I don't give a damn which side you're working for. It has nothing to do with me. Now get out of my apartment and don't ever come back!''

''Because of his defection, he had to go undercover at once and assume a new identity,'' the woman explained calmly, ignoring Meg's outburst. ''Out of fear of placing you and your daughter in danger, he has been living apart from you for the past five years and has avoided making contact until—''

''Until he could trap us in a public place where I didn't dare upset my daughter. Who's just old enough to be seduced by the attention of a long-lost father,'' Meg said bitterly.

The man shook his head. ''Not until the threat of danger had passed and he'd established himself fully in his new life.'' He paused. ''Now Mr. Rudenko has done exactly that. He's written several books on Russia already, including an exposé of the KGB and its methods. That one's coming out in the spring, under an assumed name, of course. The publisher's expecting it to make the *Times* list. So he's doing well financially, and he'll be able to support you and Anna.''

''I don't want to hear any more. Just get out. Now!''

''When you've cooled off enough to ask questions, phone Senator Strickland's office and he'll tell you everything you want to know.''

Senator Strickland? The face of the aging Missouri senator came to mind. He was a politician whose integrity had never been questioned, at least as far as Meg knew. Which didn't mean much. Senator Strickland could probably be bought as easily as the next man.

"Perhaps you don't realize he's on the Senate Foreign Relations Committee and has been cooperating with us since 1988. He knows all about your love affair with Mr. Rudenko and the daughter you conceived during your stay in the Soviet Union. We can assure you that he's your friend and that he's sympathetic to your situation. He expects to hear from you in the near future."

Meg felt the blood drain from her face. If by the most remote chance they were telling the truth, then not only the KGB but the CIA and her own state senator knew the most intimate details of her private life! The idea was so appalling Meg couldn't think, couldn't speak.

The woman eyed her for a long moment. "Ms. Roberts, your fear and distrust are entirely understandable, which is why Mr. Rudenko asked us to speak to you—to help you accept that he's a citizen now and wants a relationship with his daughter."

"You've spoken to me," Meg muttered through stiff lips. "Consider your mission accomplished."

In a few swift strides she reached the door and flung it open, anxious to be rid of the pair and desperate to get Anna to bed before Kon could exert any more influence over her. But the happy sounds of Anna's excited chatter and her father's deep laughter coming from the kitchen mocked Meg's determination to bring this cozy situation to an immediate and permanent end.

She watched till the two agents were out of sight, then quietly shut the door and slipped across the hall to ring Mrs. Rosen's bell. She prayed Kon wouldn't choose that moment to check up on her.

When there was no answer, Meg panicked. She would have started for the Garretts' apartment down the corridor, but didn't dare leave her own apartment unguarded. Besides, the sound of her daughter's tearful voice checked her movements.

Through the closed door she could hear Anna asking Kon if "those people" had made her mommy go to work. Meg didn't wait to hear his response and hurried back into the apartment, her only thought to comfort her daughter.

"Mommy!" Anna cried when she saw Meg. She ran over to her, her distress vanishing instantly. "Where did you go? We got dinner all ready!"

"I think your mother was just saying goodbye to the Bowmans at the elevator. Isn't that right?" He supplied the plausible excuse faster than Meg could think. In an unguarded moment her troubled gaze flew to his. The triumphant expression in those blue depths said he understood exactly what she'd been up to, but that she'd never be rid of him, so why not accept her fate gracefully.

"Come on, Mommy. We're hungry."

Anna tugged at Meg's hand, forcing her to break eye contact with Kon. He followed them into the kitchen at a leisurely pace. Her plan to talk to her attorney would have to be put off until dinner was over.

Whether intentionally or not, Kon's hands brushed against her shoulders as he pulled out a chair for her. She despised the tremor that shook her body when he touched her, afraid he could feel it. But to her relief his attention was focused on Anna. He helped her sit down at the small dinette table, where a plate of cheesy macaroni and broccoli and a glass of milk had been placed for each of them.

"We have to have a blessing first," Anna insisted as soon as her father sat down on her other side. "It's your turn to say it, Daddy. Please?"

"I'd be honored," he murmured in a husky voice, squeezing her small hand in his large one.

Meg forgot to close her eyes as she watched the two identical dark heads bow while he offered a prayer in Russian—a beautiful, very personal prayer that thanked God for preserving the lives of the woman and child he loved, for uniting them at last, for giving him the opportunity to start a new life, for providing food when so many people in Russia and the rest of the world had none. And finally for bringing the three of them this first Christmas together. Amen.

"What did you say, Daddy?" Anna asked, picking up her spoon and scooping up the macaroni.

He lifted his head and stared at his daughter. "I told God how happy I was finally to be with you and your mommy."

Her mouth full of macaroni, Anna declared, "Melanie says it's stupid to believe in God. Wait till I tell her that God let you come to Amerca to be with Mommy and me. I love you, Daddy."

Anna's comments and sweet smile—even more endearing because of the cheese sauce clinging to her lips—combined with the eloquent emotion darkening his eyes was too much for Meg. She found it difficult to maintain the same degree of anger she'd felt before they'd sat down to eat.

His unexpected display of reverence had sounded amazingly sincere. For a brief moment, Meg had been in danger of forgetting that everything Kon did was part of an act. An act that over the years had become second nature to him.

Was it possible he *did* have religious convictions which he'd been forced to hide until now? Could he fake something like that? She didn't know.

His glance switched to Meg. "Did we do the macaroni right?" he asked quietly. "Anna helped me make it. Our little girl is a good cook."

"And a tired one," Meg remarked without answering his question. Tearing her gaze from his, she brushed a stray curl from her daughter's flushed cheek. "I think we'll skip dessert and go straight to bed. You've had a big day, honey."

Anna nodded, surprising Meg who'd been prepared for an argument. "Daddy said I had to go to bed early and get a good sleep so I'd be ready for our trip in the morning."

Trip? What trip? Dear Lord!

Adrenaline set Meg's heart pounding like waves crashing against the shore. Her eyes darted wildly to Kon. He had just finished his milk and eyed her over the rim of the glass, registering her fear with a calm that roused her emotions to a violent pitch.

"Since tomorrow is Sunday, it will be the perfect opportunity for you and Anna to see where I live. It's a two-hour drive from here."

Meg sucked in a breath and pushed away from the table like an automaton. Refusing to let him bait her any further, she turned to Anna and said, ''If you're finished, let's run to the bathroom and brush your teeth.''

''But I want Daddy to help me. He promised to tuck me in bed. He's going to teach me how to read my *Nutcracker* book in Russian, and I'm going to read him my Dr. Seuss stories.''

''Then I'll do the dishes,'' she said, forcing her voice to remain level. She refused to give Kon the satisfaction of knowing his unexpected appearance had knocked out her underpinnings.

She ignored his curious stare, kissed Anna's forehead and started clearing the table. Acting as if she didn't have a care in the world, she set about loading the dishwasher while they got up from the table and left the kitchen.

By the time she'd wiped off the counters and watered the large red poinsettia her boss had sent her, the apartment was quiet. Removing her high heels, she turned out the kitchen light, then stole across the living room and down the hall, listening for voices.

Meg caught snatches of Anna reading Dr. Seuss's *Inside, Outside, Upside Down.* Occasionally Kon would stop her and make her pronounce the Russian equivalent of the words. Her accent appeared to entertain him no end, and he taught her some more, sometimes laughing deep in his throat at her efforts, but more often than not praising her, calling her his darling Anochka. Eventually there were no more sounds.

Meg shivered as she remembered the times she'd lain in his arms, unable to get enough of his lovemaking, never wanting him to stop calling her his beloved. But it had all been a lie, and the pain of his betrayal was more real than ever. Sweat beaded her hairline.

She entered Anna's bedroom on tiptoe and moved past the aquarium and dresser toward the twin bed. Kon was stretched out on top of the covers, his eyes closed, his arm around the child. She lay under her Winnie the Pooh quilt and had fallen asleep against his broad shoulder, several books, including the *Nutcracker,* still scattered on the bed.

The reading light fastened to the white headboard outlined Kon's features. They looked more chiseled in repose and revealed new lines of experience around his eyes and mouth. She leaned over to study him more closely.

He looked tired, she thought, then berated herself for feeling any compassion or noticing the small physical changes in him since they'd last been to-gether—changes that made him look more appealing than ever. She couldn't allow herself to respond to that appeal or to soften in any way.

Because he was planning to steal Anna.

She couldn't forget that for a second. Right now, with Kon asleep, was the perfect time to alert Ben Avery. He could start proceedings to have Kon legally removed from the apartment. No matter how much it would upset Anna, Meg needed to do this, and she needed to do it immediately. There was no way she would allow Kon to step one foot outside the door with her daughter.

Quietly she retraced her steps to the kitchen and lifted the receiver of the wall phone to call her attorney.

She gasped when she heard a sudden movement behind her. She swung around to face Kon, who stood between the living room and the kitchen, far too close for her peace of mind.

He hadn't been asleep at all!

Heat seemed to pour from her body when she realized what that meant—he'd been watching her the whole time she'd been in Anna's room. No doubt when she'd leaned close to study him while he lay there on the bed exhausted, he'd been aware of her conflicting emotions, and the knowledge compounded her anger.

Anna might think of him as Prince Marzipan, but to Meg he was a devil prince, painfully handsome in a dark, saturnine way. The faint glow from the Christmas tree lights seemed only to emphasize it.

"Whomever you're calling to come and take me away will have to kill me first. I'm here to be with my daughter. But you're Anna's mother, which gives you the ultimate power." His voice trailed off.

Like someone in a trance, Meg hung up the receiver and stared at him, her fear and pain so acute she couldn't swallow. "Maybe that was true, once. But this afternoon you presented Anna with a fait accompli." She spoke haltingly, the tears welling up in her eyes. "How could you have been so...rash? So insensitive? What you told Anna—your declaration of fatherhood—has changed our lives forever!"

"I hope so," he said in a hoarse whisper.

Her hands knotted into fists. "I won't let you take her back to Russia!" she cried. "I'll do whatever I have to do to prevent that from happening. *Whatever I have to do,*" she warned him a second time.

"Your imagination is as predictable as your paranoia, but I have no intention of kidnapping her. Our daughter would despise me forever if I took her away from you. That is hardly the emotion I want to evoke in my one and only child. Besides, I'm very much afraid that Konstantin Rudenko is persona non grata in the former Soviet Union these days.

"If I were to touch the trees of Mother Russia just one more time," he murmured in a faraway voice, "it would be my last act as a free man." A mirthless smile broke the corner of his mouth. "I have no desire to deprive my daughter of her father. Not when I've spent the last six years in near isolation making plans and preparations—so we can live the rest of our lives together, Meggie."

CHAPTER THREE

MEGGIE. The name he called her the first time he'd kissed her...

Suddenly she was that naive, starry-eyed twenty-three-year-old, sitting in the front seat of Kon's black Mercedes as he drove her from the Moscow airport to the hotel in St. Petersburg where she'd be living for the next four months.

Already infatuated with Konstantin Rudenko long before she'd arrived in Russia the second time, she knew she was in love the minute she set eyes on him again. The austere, heart-stoppingly attractive KGB agent had been assigned to guard her and escort her to and from school. Her feelings for him had been growing ever since he'd rescued her from prison on her first trip, giving her that beautiful book....

As before, his word was law and everyone jumped at his slightest dictate. He'd dealt with all the red tape and smoothed her way, making her feel safe and looked after rather than policed. To add to her happiness, she'd learned that part of his duty was to phone her room every morning between three and four o'clock to make sure she hadn't slipped away from the hotel unnoticed.

Being a foreigner on the loose in a Russian city constituted a crime punishable by imprisonment, something she had no desire to repeat.

Once installed at the hotel, Meg couldn't wait for his nightly phone calls to begin. But a problem arose when she discovered she'd been given a middle-aged roommate, a Mrs. Procter who had a master's in Russian from a university in Illinois. Meg was crushed because it meant that any phone conversations with Mr. Rudenko could be overheard by her roommate.

He, like the agent assigned to Mrs. Procter, would phone and ask her, very formally, if all was well, then start to hang up. But Meg couldn't let him end the calls there, and for the first few nights had tried to engage him in conversation by discussing her students' papers with him—anything she could think of to prolong the contact.

After a few days she'd managed to keep him on the phone as long as fifteen or twenty minutes, occasionally touching on the personal, learning that his first name was Konstantin. But Meg wanted much more from Kon, as she'd secretly nicknamed him, than a nightly phone call. But for that, she needed privacy, which Mrs. Procter's presence made impossible.

The older woman was scandalized by Meg's behavior and expressed her disapproval of what she referred to as Meg's "promiscuous" character. It didn't take long for Meg to realize she couldn't take much more of the unpleasant woman's attitude or presence.

Most important, she couldn't bear it when Kon just drove off at the end of each day after depositing her at the hotel, never lingering to chat for even a few more minutes.

By the end of the second week, Meg had craved his company to the point that she started plotting ways to get him to spend more time with her. That Friday, when he'd pulled up in the parking spot designated for KGB by the hotel, she didn't immediately get out of the car.

With her heart in her throat, she turned to him. Her gaze feasted on his slightly-too-long hair and the searing blue of his eyes, eyes that never revealed his innermost thoughts or feelings.

"If you don't mind, t-there's something important I need to discuss with you. Since the hotel frowns on my being late for dinner, I was hoping you'd join me. Or better yet," she continued in a slightly breathless voice, "I was hoping you might take me to a restaurant, where we could talk in private. So far I've only eaten at the hotel, and I'm eager to see more of the city while I'm here."

A frown marred his handsome features. "What is the problem?" he asked in a businesslike tone, which was hardly encouraging.

"I-it's about my accommodations."

"They are not up to your American standards?"

"No. It's nothing like that. Maybe it's because I've never had to live with a roommate before. But I'm afraid Mrs. Procter and I don't get along too well. We're such different ages and . . . I was wondering if I could be given a room by myself. I don't care if it's small, and I'd be willing to pay extra for it. All I'd really like is my privacy." *And the opportunity to talk to you all night long, if you'll let me.*

He cocked his head and studied her gravely. She would have given anything to know what he was really thinking. "Come," he said unexpectedly. "Let's go inside. While you eat your dinner, I'll see what can be done."

Her heart leapt. At least he hadn't said no. Elated by that much progress, Meg alighted from the car and entered the hotel with Kon at her heels. While he approached the clerk at the front desk, she hurried to her room on the second floor to deposit her briefcase and freshen up.

So excited she was trembling, Meg applied fresh lipstick and dabbed on some French perfume, then slipped into a coffee-toned silk dress that had a tailored elegance. She brushed her ash-blond hair till it gleamed and fell softly about her shoulders, all the while praying he would find her attractive enough to join her in the dining room for a meal. Their first together...

But her heart plummeted to her feet when she went downstairs to the lobby and was greeted instead by the desk clerk. He informed her that a new room on the third floor had been arranged for her, that she should eat her dinner, then transfer her personal belongings.

Though grateful for Kon's swift help and intervention, she couldn't hide her disappointment; he'd left without saying goodbye. No longer interested in dinner, she went back upstairs ahead of Mrs. Procter, who was at one of the tables in the dining room talking to another teacher from England. No doubt they were gossiping about Meg.

Thankful to be free of that woman, Meg moved everything out of the room before Mrs. Procter learned what had happened and asked a lot of probing questions.

The interior of the tacky, modern hotel was drab and uninteresting, but her new room turned out to be considerably larger than the first one. It contained a good-sized desk with a lamp where she could do her schoolwork. Once again, she was touched by Kon's thoughtfulness and consideration. She could hardly wait until he phoned her that night to thank him.

When she heard a rap on the door, she whirled around, assuming it was one of the hotel staff. But before she had time to reach for the handle, the door opened.

She gasped softly when she saw Kon standing there. He'd never come to her room before. Her heart started to race. Their eyes met and she saw something flicker in his gaze as it swept over her face and body, something that made her go hot and liquefied her bones.

He wasn't indifferent to her. She could see it, feel it.

"Will the room do?" he asked in a husky voice.

She had difficulty finding words. "Yes," she finally managed. "It's perfect. Thank you."

He stared at her through half-closed lids. "There's a club not far from here where we can go for a drink and you can see something of the nightlife. I could spare an hour if you wish."

She swallowed hard. "I do."

"The nights are cold now. Wear something warm."

Scarcely able to breathe with the emotions running rampant inside her, she turned toward the closet for her raincoat.

"I'll wait for you at the car."

She glanced back in time to see him disappear down the dimly lit hallway. A club meant there might be dancing. The need to touch him, to be held in his arms, was fast growing into a permanent ache.

Within seconds she was ready and practically flew down the two flights of stairs and through the lobby, not wanting to waste one precious moment. As she emerged, her eyes went straight to his. She knew her cheeks were flushed with a feverish excitement she couldn't hide.

He was standing next to his car, his hands in his coat pockets—a remote, solitary figure. Evidently he'd been keeping an eye on the entrance, because as soon as he saw her, he stepped forward and opened the passenger door.

Without saying a word, he started the engine and they pulled away from the curb into moderate evening traffic, driving alongside bikes and trolley cars. Meg loved St. Petersburg, called the "Venice of the North" because of its waterways and bridges. Maybe the city looked so beautiful that night because she'd been fantasizing about the man who sat an arm's length away from her. She could hardly believe they were going out together. If she had her way, it would be longer than one hour. Far longer...

He obviously knew the city well. He took them through several narrow, winding alleyways before pulling to a stop behind some expensive-looking cars parked next to a cluster of old buildings.

Her pulse racing, she watched him come around to help her from the car, something he'd always done. But this time there was a subtle difference. This time she felt his hand go to the back of her waist as he guided her through the first set of doors. She could hear sixties' music, of all things, being played inside the building.

His lips twitched in a half smile, transforming the austere-looking KGB agent into the devastatingly attractive man she'd been dreaming about. "You're surprised."

"You knew I would be." She smiled back, so enamored of him, she felt giddy.

"We're not quite as stodgy as propaganda would have you believe."

After helping her remove her coat, which he checked with an attendent, he ushered her through an ornate bar area to another room, where couples were dancing to a live band. The talented musicians and singer made her feel as if they'd just walked into a New York nightclub.

Out of the corner of her eye she saw Kon give the waiter a signal. The man rushed over and within seconds, they were escorted to a free table. Kon said something privately to the waiter, who then left them alone.

Kon seated her, then pulled out the chair opposite. He eyed her with a hint of speculation. "Do you trust me to have ordered something I believe you'll like?"

She lifted solemn eyes to him. "Because of you, I was freed from that awful jail and able to get home in time for my father's funeral. I'd trust you with my life." She spoke with complete and heartfelt sincerity.

For once, something she said managed to penetrate that outer KGB shell and reach the man beneath. She could tell by the way his eyes darkened in color, and the sudden stillness that came over him.

The band started playing an old Beatles tune.

"Let's dance," he murmured in a low voice.

Meg had been waiting for those words. She followed him onto the floor on shaky legs, so eager to be in his arms, she was almost afraid of the moment he'd touch her, afraid he'd know the powerful effect he had on her.

Perhaps he did know how she felt, because to her chagrin he kept her at a correct distance, never taking advantage of their closeness in any way, or letting her think her nearness disturbed him.

Like many of his compatriots in the room, he was a wonderful dancer, and their bodies seemed perfectly attuned. After three dances they returned to their table, where she discovered champagne cocktails and goblets of ice cream that tasted more like lime sherbet.

"What a delicious combination," she marveled, realizing that the entire evening felt enchanted because she was in love with him.

Thirsty from the dancing, Meg drank her cocktail quickly. Then she looked across at him, wondering what he could be thinking to produce such a sober expression. Anxious to lighten his mood, she leaned toward him. "Shall we dance again?" She hoped her question didn't sound too much like begging.

"There's no more time," he told her with a cool, disappointing finality. "I'll get your coat while you finish your ice cream."

She didn't want the evening to end, but had little choice in the matter. He was in charge. Meg supposed it was something of a miracle that he'd taken even an hour from his rigid routine to accommodate her wishes.

"Shall we go?"

She nodded and pushed herself away from the table. They made their way through the crowd to the entrance. This time he didn't touch her as they stepped outside to walk the short distance to his car. In fact, there was a distinct difference between the way Kon treated her now—almost as if he were angry—and the way he'd responded to her earlier in the evening. Was it because he'd revealed something of the man beneath the KGB persona? Maybe now he wanted to show her that it had only been a momentary aberration, that she shouldn't expect it to happen again.

Once they were in the car, driving back to her hotel, Meg didn't speak. The forbidding aura surrounding him prevented her from initiating further conversation. She stared out the side window, dreading the moment he'd say good-night and walk away.

They were almost at their destination when he suddenly made a right turn out of the city, away from lighted streets into darkness.

"Kon? W-where are we going? This isn't the way back to the hotel." But he refused to answer her and pressed forward until they were well into the woods. She started to feel nervous. "I thought you had to get back to... to whatever it is you do."

Still he ignored her and kept driving until they came to a deserted lay-by. He turned off the road and pulled to a stop, cutting the engine. The only sound she could hear was the fierce hammering of her own heart.

Glancing outside, she noticed trees lining the road and saw the stars twinkling overhead. The beauty of the night did not escape her, but she couldn't concentrate on that now. The man at the wheel had become an enigmatic stranger, and she was very much at his mercy.

When she couldn't stand the silence any longer, she turned toward him. The shadowy light from the dashboard revealed the look in his eyes, an unmistakable longing that changed the rhythm of her heart.

"Are you afraid of me?"

"No," she answered in a tremulous voice. And it was the truth.

He let out a smothered curse. "You should be. In the last six years, you've changed from a lovely, spirited teenager into an exciting woman. My comrades envy me because I chose to guard you myself."

She moistened her lips, gratified to hear the unmistakably possessive ring in his voice. "I-I'm glad you did. It saved me the trouble of looking for you."

"Explain that remark."

Meg stared down at her hands. "Just that I've never forgotten your kindness to me. I intended to look you up and thank you. And—I hoped—get to know you better."

She heard his sharp intake of breath. "Your honesty is as shocking now as it was six years ago."

She lifted her head, half turning to face him. "You said that as if it offends you."

"On the contrary, I find it refreshing beyond belief. Will it shock you senseless if I tell you how much I want to make love to you, go to bed with you? How much I want to kiss every inch of your face and hair, your beautiful body?"

At those words, she couldn't control the trembling. "No," she murmured, looking into his eyes, "because I've wanted the same thing since I got off the plane in Moscow."

Groaning, he said, "Come here to me." He reached out to pull her into his arms, but she was already there.

"Meggie." She heard him whisper her name before his mouth fastened on hers. He kissed her with a hunger that obliterated any fears she might have entertained that he wasn't as attracted to her as she was to him.

Overjoyed by the knowledge, she clung to his warmth, kissing him with total abandon, letting sensation after sensation carry her to unexplored dimensions of wanting and need. She'd craved this physical closeness for so long, she was afraid they were both part of a dream. She never wanted to wake up.

In her bemused state she wasn't aware of time passing. Nor did she notice the eventual glare of headlights coming in their direction—until they flashed inside the car.

With a speed and strength she could scarcely grasp, Kon thrust her back to her side of the car, her lipstick nonexistent, her face hot, her body throbbing.

By the time the other vehicle had driven past them, Kon started the engine and pulled onto the road, maneuvering the car with the same finesse and precision that he did everything else, his features schooled to show no emotion.

"Kon— I—I don't want to go back. I don't want the night to end. Please don't take me home yet."

"I have to, Meggie."

"Because of your job?"

"Yes."

"When can we be together again? Really together, for more than an hour?"

"I'll work something out."

"Please let it be soon."

"Don't say anything else, Meggie, and don't touch me again tonight."

His emotions were as explosive as hers. For once, she didn't mind that he was taking her back to the hotel, not when she knew his passion for her was as profound as hers was for him. His unnatural silence after what they'd just shared proved there was no going back to their former relationship.

When they reached the hotel, he remained at the wheel and let her get out on her own. The moment she was safely inside, he sped away, as if in pursuit of another car.

Meg dashed through the foyer and up the stairs, thankful to be going to an empty room. At least she could relive the rapture of the night in total privacy.

But long after she'd showered, brushed her teeth and gone to bed, she lay wide-awake. The adrenaline seemed to pulse through her bloodsteam; she couldn't sleep. The phone was right by the bed and she turned on her side, waiting for his call.

When it came, she'd grabbed the receiver before the second ring.

"Kon?" she cried out joyously.

"Never answer the phone that way again."

Chastened, she whispered, "I'm sorry. I didn't think."

"It's already Saturday. Be ready at ten and pack some warm clothes for the weekend." The line went dead.

Meg put back the receiver and hugged her pillow, delirious with love and longing. Sleep would be impossible now.

To keep from watching the clock, she got out her homework and made up her lesson plans for the following week. When she'd finished that task, she graded her students' poetry, writing notes at the bottom of each paper.

Work was a godsend; it kept her busy until nine, when she put everything away and packed the things she'd need for their trip. At nine-thirty, she left her room and went downstairs to breakfast, nodding to the few teachers she knew. She breathed a sigh of relief that Mrs. Procter wasn't among them.

Promptly at ten, Kon entered the foyer. She felt his powerful presence even before she saw him—like a gravitational pull. She hurried toward him, carrying her overnight bag in one hand, her purse in the other.

To any passerby, he would have looked like the same KGB agent who'd been ferrying her back and forth since her arrival in St. Petersburg. The difference was apparent only to Meg. When Kon gazed at her in that special way, she felt an emotional and physical awareness she couldn't hide. She felt a sensation of falling helplessly toward him, unable to stop.

He couldn't have had much sleep, either, but the relaxed mouth and the darkness beneath his eyes gave him a slightly dissipated air that only added to his attractiveness. Meekly, she followed him to his car and got in while he stowed her bag in the trunk.

They headed out of the city in much the same direction they'd taken the night before. The traffic lightened, and soon after, they reached the forest road.

Meg turned in her seat, admiring his striking profile, and his tautly muscled body. He was as formally dressed as always. In fact, she'd never seen him in anything but a white shirt and dark suit—his uniform, she supposed. He wore it well. Too well. She couldn't keep her eyes off him. "I've never gone away with a man before," she confessed. "H-have you? Gone away with a woman, I mean."

He flashed her a brief but piercing glance. "Yes."

"I should never have asked that question, but this is all new to me."

Naturally he'd had affairs. She knew from their nightly conversations that he was in his early thirties. An unattached male as attractive as Kon would never be without female companionship.

"There haven't been as many women as your fertile imagination is conjuring up," he said in a gently mocking voice. "My work makes it virtually impossible to sustain any kind of lasting relationship. The few women I've known also worked for the Party.

"If it means anything, Meggie, I've never been attracted to a non-Russian woman before. What surprises me is the strength of my feelings for you, how far I've been willing to go to get you alone."

She shivered with excitement. "Th-thank you for being honest with me. If we can have that, I won't ask for anything else."

His long fingers tightened on the steering wheel. "You've never made love with a man, have you." It was a statement, not a question.

"No. Does that make a difference to you?"

"Yes."

She blinked to fight the sudden sting of tears. "I see."

He muttered something in Russian she couldn't quite catch. "We're here, Meggie."

She'd been so caught up in their conversation, she hadn't noticed anything else. Now when she turned her head, she could see they were in the middle of a dense wood, parked outside what could only be described as a lowly woodcutter's cottage.

The reality of the situation came to her with full force. She'd hoped her candor would be enough to make up for her inexperience, but now she knew differently. Kon was a tough, sophisticated, worldly man—and he was probably ready to turn around and take her back to the city.

She couldn't bear that. She bolted suddenly from the car, taking off into the woods.

"Meggie? Where do you think you're going?" he called after her, sounding cxaspcratcd.

"I-I'll be right back."

"Don't go too far. It's easy to get lost."

"I won't." *Just give me a moment to pull myself together,* she cried inwardly and kept on running until she was out of breath.

She flung herself against a tree trunk to rest. She felt a rush of embarrassment because she was behaving like anything but a mature woman. She wouldn't blame him if he'd lost complete interest.

That was when she heard him calling her. He sounded angry, upset. Maybe he believed the woman he'd assigned himself to guard had managed to give him the slip. If only he knew the truth—that she *never* wanted to be apart from him. Never.

From the sound of his voice, he was getting closer. If she wasn't mistaken, his tone conveyed real anxiety. Did she dare believe he was actually concerned for her? Could he possibly have feelings for her as deep and as real as those she had for him?

The answer came when he caught up with her as she hurried back toward the hut. "I'm sorry if I worried you," she said when she saw his chest heaving and heard a torrent of unintelligible Russian escape lips narrowed to a taut, uncompromising line.

In the next instant he reached for her, drawing her against his hard body, his eyes a scorching flame of blue.

"*Meggie . . .*"

The fierceness, the unexpected raw passion in his outcry, robbed her of breath, telling her what she needed to know. He still wanted to be with her. Nothing had changed.

Blindly she lifted her mouth for his kiss—and was lost. He picked her up in his arms and carried her into the hut, shoving the door closed with his boot.

Her heart streamed into his, and what happened next felt completely natural and inevitable. Drunk on her desire for him, she forgot they were anything but a man and a woman, aching to know the taste and feel of each other.

From that moment on, the barriers imposed by their roles as foreign visitor and KGB agent were cast aside. Their all-consuming need for each other had dictated their relationship. A need that found release and marked the beginning of the rest of their days and nights together. The only thing they'd wanted was to love each other into oblivion....

To think it had all been part of a game plan.

Meg shook off the memories. She thought she'd put that pain behind her forever. But Kon's takeover since his reappearance in her life and Anna's had reopened wounds that would never heal now. She stared at him with accusing eyes.

"Tell me something," she said, not bothering to hide her reaction to the bittersweet memories. "How did you manage to keep a straight face when you asked me to be your wife?"

"Which time was that, Meggie?" he asked quietly. "As I recall, I begged you to marry me every time we made love. Perhaps I should ask *you* a question. Whatever possessed me to keep asking you when I knew what your answer would be?" He managed to sound as desolate as he had earlier, when he'd told Anna about his parting scene at the airport before Meg flew away from him.

He was good at this! He was so good, it terrified her.

"Spare me the deceit, Kon!" She spoke scornfully to mask her uncertainty. "You're a man who did a job for your country. Throughout your career, I'm sure you've managed to infatuate other unsuspecting female visitors like myself. Perhaps you've even fathered other children in the line of duty—" She stopped suddenly, breathless with anger.

"Why seek out Anna when there are thousands of single women in Russia who would love to marry you and bear your child? From what I understand, women there far outnumber men. You could choose anyone you wanted and have a family if—"

Calmly he interrupted. "The woman I've chosen is standing right in front of me, and the child I already have fell asleep in my arms only moments ago."

She clenched her teeth. "You *did* choose me, I'll grant you that. My uncle was in naval intelligence, remember? And after he died my aunt told me about the KGB and the way they tried to convert specially chosen foreign visitors. Like me—the niece of an American military officer. Especially since I was obviously interested in Russia and even came back a second time.

"You did everything by the book, Kon. And with all your charm, you came close to succeeding. You tried to woo me away from my country by first befriending me, then seducing me. But in the end, it didn't work. I still went back to the States, and you were probably reprimanded for your failure. So you had me watched, and when you found out I was pregnant, you waited and plotted until the time was right to claim your daughter and return to Russia."

She could tell her voice was getting louder, but she was fast losing control. "Well, I'm not going to let you do it! We're not married, and if you try to take her anywhere, I'll have you brought up on kidnap—"

"Mommy!" Anna's frightened cry shocked Meg into silence. Stunned by the interruption, she looked past Kon to see her daughter hovering near the Christmas tree, hugging her favorite doll. The glint of tears on her pale cheeks devastated Meg. "Why are you mad at my daddy?"

Kon moved so fast Meg didn't have time to blink. In one lithe move he gathered Anna in his arms and kissed her nose. "She's not mad at me, Anochka," he assured her while he rocked her back and forth. "Your mommy is upset, with good reason. I used to live in Russia, and she's afraid that one day I'll want to go back and take you with me."

"Without *mommy?*" Anna asked, as if the idea was unthinkable. Meg was moved to tears.

"No one is going anywhere without Mommy," he stated with unmistakable authority, his eyes never leaving Meg. She wondered how he could carry play-acting this far and still sound so convincing. She watched him kiss the top of Anna's head.

"Now it's time for you to go back to bed, because we've got a big day planned for tomorrow, and your mommy and I haven't finished talking yet. You know we've been apart a long time. There are things I need to tell her. Can you understand that? Are you old enough to run to your room and crawl under the covers by yourself?"

"Yes." Anna nodded, making the dark curls dance on her forehead. Her head swiveled around and her eyes, full of pleading, fastened on Meg. "Daddy loves us, Mommy. Can we go see our house tomorrow? The dogs are waiting for me."

Meg stared at her daughter in wonder. How simple it all appeared to Anna's trusting mind. How pure her faith. She didn't know the meaning of real fear or betrayal. Those emotions weren't within her experience—how could she comprehend them? Now that her beloved prince, her daddy, had actually materialized, her child's world was complete.

"I live in Hannibal." He offered the surprising revelation so quietly it was as if his mind had spoken to Meg's.

"It's in the state of Missouri," he added dryly. "It's famous as the home of Mark Twain."

That provoked her to say, "Next you'll be telling me Mark Twain is still alive and entertaining friends at his house on Hill Street."

He gave Anna another hug. "Interesting you'd mention Hill Street. I live farther up the hill on the same side of the street."

It seemed the fairy tale was never ending. A KGB agent in the land of Becky Thatcher and Huck Finn.

Meg let out an angry laugh and folded her arms to prevent herself from flinging something at him. "Anna, it's long past your bedtime."

"She's right," Kon agreed. "Kiss me good-night, Anochka."

Meg refused to watch their display of affection and turned on her heel, heading for Anna's room. She was unable to credit the fact that less than eight hours ago Anna hadn't known her father's name, let alone imagined seeing him in the flesh.

She stood by the side of the bed until her daughter scrambled beneath the quilt, but she couldn't avoid the innocent blue eyes staring into her soul. "God sent Daddy to us. Aren't you happy, Mommy? Please be happy."

Meg sagged onto the mattress and buried her face in Anna's neck, hugging her daughter close. "Oh, honey—" she began to sob quietly "—if only it was that simple." Convulsion after convulsion racked Meg's body, and Anna's comforting pats only contributed to her debilitating weakness.

"It *is* that simple," a deep, masculine voice said from the doorway. "And we're *all* going to be happy."

CHAPTER FOUR

THE NEXT THING Meg knew, his hand was sliding into her hair and caressing her scalp. It sent a shock wave through her system. Her breath caught, and she released Anna. She was so shaken by his touch she got to her feet and fled from the room in fresh panic.

Kon followed more slowly. "You're tired, Meggie. Go to bed. I'll sleep on the couch. If Anna wakes up during the night, I'll take care of her."

Meg spun around, the cathartic release of pent-up emotion making her feel reckless. But her desire to get everything out in the open diminished when she faced him in her stocking feet. Next to him she felt small and physically weak, emotionally overwhelmed. He seemed even taller, darker and infinitely more dangerous than before.

"Why, Kon?" she blurted, fighting the attraction that was still there in all the old insidious ways. "Why have you really come? Don't tell me it's because you're in love with me. We both know that's a lie. You used me!" she accused him. "I-I'll admit I was the aggressor. In fact, I threw myself at you and made your job pathetically easy. Because of my naïveté, I'll go on paying for that for the rest of my life.

"But why make up stories that will only devastate a vulnerable little girl? If you're really telling the truth and you *have* defected, then the only reason I can imagine for any of this is that you hope to get joint custody—to keep Anna to yourself for six months every year. I couldn't bear that. Do you hear me?"

Her question rang in the air, but for once he didn't have a ready response. While she waited, he lowered himself to the couch and ran his hands through his hair, a gesture she remembered from countless occasions in the past. It drew her attention to his fit, lithe body, which at one time had known hers so intimately....

She shook her head, furious that she could entertain such primitive thoughts when he was more her enemy now than ever before.

Deep in contemplation, she scarcely noticed that he'd pulled a pocket-size tape recorder out of his suit jacket. He placed it on the round marble-topped coffee table, one of the few pieces of furniture she'd kept after her parents had died—one of the few good pieces they'd owned. Her father's schoolteacher salary hadn't supplied much more than the necessities of life. Without winning scholarships, Meg would never have been able to go abroad in the first place.

Suddenly the sound of hysterical sobbing filled the living room. Meg blinked in shock when she recognized her own teenage voice. Her eyes flew to Kon, whose head was bent over the recorder, listening.

Immediately Meg was transported back to that dank Moscow jail cell. She remembered beating the stone floor with her fists in abject despair. The agony of that black moment came rushing in, overwhelming her with its intensity, and she couldn't stop the tears from streaming down her face.

Oh, Daddy. You're gone…my daddy's gone…. I've got to get home to you! They've got to let me out of here! Let me out of here, you monsters…. Daddy…!

To be confronted by her own screams, her own sorrow, was too much to bear. Without conscious thought she flew at Kon, but he'd already pressed the stop button. "Why would you have kept that tape?" She clutched at his arm, shaking him, forcing him to look at her. "What are you trying to do to me? How could you be so cruel?" she lashed out, uncaring that her tears were wetting his shirt.

Catching her off guard, he pulled her onto his lap. He gripped her face in his hands, preventing her from thrashing about by trapping her legs between his. With a gentle stroke of his thumbs, he smoothed the moisture from her lashes. "When I instructed the guard to play back the tape for me and I heard your relentless sobbing, it released a memory buried so deep in my psyche I didn't know it was there until that moment."

His breath warmed her face, but she was too distraught to realize the danger of being this close to him again.

"What memory?"

His body tautened. "Of an icy-cold morning when two men came to my schoolroom in Siberia and told me I was to go with them, that my mother needed me at home. I was eight years old. I remember that very distinctly because my father, who worked with his hands, had made me a sled for my birthday. I loved my father and was very proud of it. In fact, I pulled it to school so I could play with it on the way home and show my friends.

"When I told the men I needed to get my sled, which the teacher had told me to put around the back of the one-room building, they said there was no time, that it would be there tomorrow. I was upset about it, but my fear that something bad had happened to my mother was foremost in my mind.

"They put me in a horse-drawn sleigh and set off in the opposite direction from my house. When I told them we were going the wrong way, one of the men slapped me and told me to be quiet. He said that the state was my family now. That I wasn't to speak about my family again or they would kill my sister and my parents."

Meg's involuntary cry went ignored by Kon. He kept on talking in the same low, steady voice. "But if I was good, they would tell my family I had gone out on the ice over the lake with my sled and had fallen through before anyone could save me."

She shook her head in disbelief. "You're making this up. You have to be," she whispered, unable to conceive of anything so horrifying. But when she dared to look into his eyes, she glimpsed an unspeakable kind of bleakness, a pain that made her heart lurch.

"I said the same thing to myself while they drove me farther and farther away from the only security I'd ever known. Then came night. They must have put me in a barn, because I was pushed into some straw and told that if I cried, they would kill me. But if I showed

I was a man, then it would prove I was worthy of the great honor they had bestowed upon me, the honor of serving the state.''

"Oh, Kon!" She broke down, overcome by the enormity of what he'd told her. For the moment the enmity between them was forgotten. She became mother, sister, lover, wanting only to give comfort to the child in him who could not be comforted. It seemed the most natural thing in the world to press her head into his neck and murmur incoherent endearments, much the same way she did when Anna needed consolation.

"I've heard stories of such things happening." She spoke against the side of his neck. "But I never wanted to believe them."

"I'd forgotten all of it," he said, brushing the silvery-blond strands of hair from her face while he rocked her in his arms, "until you were detained. Then your pain became my pain and I couldn't distinguish between them, couldn't tell the difference. It was in my power to keep you incarcerated as long as I desired, regardless of your grief. You'd broken the law and deserved to be punished. That was what I believed. That was part of the KGB's bullying tactics." He gave a deep, shuddering sigh. "But when I heard you call out for your daddy, something inside me snapped. I had to let you go."

The rocking stopped and his haunted eyes met hers. "No child, young or old, should be made to suffer the kind of night I was forced to endure in that barn, knowing I'd never see my family again. Knowing I'd never hear my mother tell me another story. Knowing

I couldn't even keep the sled my father had just made for me. Not allowed even the smallest memento of the family I'd loved."

He was telling her the truth, Meg knew. A strangled sound escaped her throat. He'd wanted to console her during that terrible night. There'd been nothing he could do then, so he'd given her the book, secretly putting it in her suitcase. During her second visit, Meg had asked him about it and he'd been noncommittal. "Just a gift," he'd said. Now she understood.

"You wouldn't explain when I asked you before," she said. "But it was because you knew how devastated I felt. How alone."

"Yes. I wanted you to leave with something you treasured, one good memory of my country. And of me..."

Meg lowered her head. "When the customs official in New York opened my suitcase, I saw it lying on top of my things. I couldn't believe it. I knew you had to have put it there, but I didn't understand why, and I couldn't figure out how you knew I wanted that particular book."

"All the staff at your hotel were KGB, Meggie. That's why the teachers and students from America were put there. It was easier for your guide to monitor your group's activities and report to me. He was careful to make notations on the kinds of things that interested you in the shops, particularly any reading material. Part of an agent's work was to seek out those visitors who might be sympathetic to Soviet communism and win them over."

Meg shuddered to think that from the time they'd arrived in Moscow until the moment Kon had rushed her to the plane, she and her friends had been collected and examined like insects under a microscope.

"He must have been disappointed when I passed up the free propaganda for a book on the *Nutcracker.* I wanted it badly but couldn't afford it."

"If anything, he was surprised. Normally American students grab at whatever is given away. Even if it's not free, they have their parents' money to squander. But you were different."

She took a steadying breath and wiped more tears from her face. "How was I different?"

"You were a lovely teenager, independent and spoiled like all of your crowd, but incredibly brave in front of the guards. So free in spirit. Young as you were, you never cowered. A part of me was intrigued by that remarkable quality in you."

She raised her head and their gazes held for a long moment until Meg stirred restlessly in his arms. She felt amazed by his confession, but more troubled and confused than ever. There could be no doubt about the nightmare he'd lived through as a child. But since the age of eight, the KGB had been his family.

Some of what he'd said today, tonight, was the truth. But which part was the lie? *And what was she doing on his lap with her body practically molded to his, their mouths only inches apart?*

Alarmed that her perspective had been clouded by compassion, she pushed her hands against his chest and struggled to her feet. She needed to separate herself from him—to fight off the sensual appeal he'd always had for her.

Something must be fundamentally wrong with her, letting him penetrate her defenses like this! It was all because he'd been able to arouse feelings that were in direct conflict with her fears.

"Your new family did a remarkable job of training you," she said coldly, attempting to put emotional distance between them. "Accosting Anna and me at the theater the way you did was a perfect example of the typical KGB takeover. It comes as naturally to you as breathing, doesn't it, Kon?

"But there's one thing you didn't know. If you try to take Anna from me, I will fight you in court. She's known only me since she was born. It would be cruel to separate us. I won't let you!"

"I've already told you that's not my intention. I want all three of us to live together." A complacent smile curved his lips. "In any event, it's too late for ultimatums, isn't it, Meggie? My daughter and I have already bonded, and I promised her I'd be here when she wakes up in the morning. Surely after spending four months in my company, you learned that I never break a promise."

"You broke *one*," she said icily. When his eyebrows rose she went on, "You'd promised I wouldn't get pregnant. I was foolish enough to believe you."

His eyes narrowed. "You and I both know I used protection. Every single time. But it appears we underestimated our little girl's determination to be born."

"No, Kon. All it means is that I underestimated how far you'd go to make it look like an accident."

His mouth thinned ominously. "Let's get something straight. The second time you came to Russia, it was not my intention to make you pregnant. If that *had* been the plan, I would have taken you to bed the day you stepped on Russian soil."

He didn't need to add that she'd been his for the asking. The humiliation she felt produced a blush she couldn't hide.

"For your information," he continued, "I had many responsibilities, of which you were only one, a quite insignificant one. I should have assigned you to a guard at the lowest echelon. In fact, it was such a routine job that one of my colleagues actually made a comment wondering why I would bother myself with anything so trivial as the surveillance of an unimportant American schoolteacher.

"I won't insult your intelligence by denying that some of the agents did sleep with their targets to obtain secrets. One of the reasons I assigned myself to you was to protect you from just such a situation."

"Why would you do that?"

He sat back against the cushions. "Because there was a refreshing innocence about you when you left Russia the first time. An honesty. Six years later, when I saw your name on a list of foreign teachers coming for a short-term stay, I wanted to see if that innocence was still there." He paused for one breathless moment.

"The only change I could see was that the teenage girl had grown into a beautiful woman. More than ever I wanted to make sure no man took advantage of you while you were in my country.''

''I don't believe you, Kon.''

He cocked his head to the side and studied her briefly. ''Did I ever once force myself on you, Meggie? Have you forgotten that you were the one who rejected me?''

Somehow their arguments always ended with his turning things around so she appeared to be the culprit. Until she met Kon, she'd never been in love. There had been no serious boyfriends in Meg's teens, no prior physical experiences to give her insight or prepare her for the full-blown emotional and sexual feelings she'd had for the man who was Anna's father.

Meg was an only child, born to a mother in her forties and a father in his fifties, both of whom were overjoyed to have a child at last. Being devout Christians who lived on a modest income, they'd sheltered her, pressured her to make the most of her studies, insisted she take advantage of every academic opportunity.

They'd been pacifists who had strongly believed in understanding as the key to world peace. In keeping with their beliefs, they'd enrolled her in a special Russian program from grade school through college. Neither of them lived long enough to realize that this well-intentioned idea would lead her down a path of forbidden passion to the life-and-death situation she faced now, in her own apartment.

''I couldn't give up my citizenship and walk away from my whole life!''

"Certainly not for me," he said beneath his breath, but she heard him and became angry all over again at his power to make her feel guilty. "So I took whatever you were willing to offer, which was as many days and nights in your arms as we could manage. I'm a man, Meggie. You know how it was with us."

"You mean you know how I thought it was with us," she said acidly. "Obviously everything was a lie! You set out to manipulate me and . . . seduce me. And you succeeded."

His gaze swept over her face and body. Oddly, it reminded her of the way he'd looked at her when she'd been detained by the airport guards.

"You're right. I did set out to win you over. But I've already told you—my success was hardly complete."

Meg, prepared for any excuse except his cold-blooded admission, felt she'd just been slapped.

"Before detente, part of my job was to keep track of foreign visitors, most of whom were tourists. Your uncle's information was correct. If any of them made a second visit, they were kept on a special list and targeted as either possible recruits or possible subversives. Special agents were assigned to scrutinize their behavior. If the same visitor came a third time, he or she was detained indefinitely."

His gaze bore into hers. "Evidently your bad experience in our jail didn't prevent you from returning, which proved what I'd thought about you—that you had an indomitable will. Intrigued by that, I made certain you were placed under my personal supervision."

Meg's head flew back. "And I was naive enough to suppose our meeting again was pure coincidence," she said angrily. "I couldn't believe my luck. Here I thought it might be impossible to track you down so I could thank you for letting me go home to my father's funeral, for giving me that book. Instead, there you were. Right at the Moscow airport!" She struggled to keep her voice steady.

"What was even more astonishing was realizing I'd been put in your charge," she went on after a moment. "In the midst of all that red tape and the endless questions, you once again whisked me away to St. Petersburg. I felt like a princess who'd been rescued by a knight in shining armor. I put you on a pedestal. Imagine putting a KGB agent on a pedestal!" she exclaimed savagely.

He heaved a deep sigh. "Can this keep till morning? I'm tired. Good night, Meggie."

Before she could say another word, he'd removed his shoes and stretched out on her couch, turning on his side so his back was toward her. The sight of him made her shake with rage.

"What do you think you're doing?"

"Shh. You'll wake Anna. I thought it was clear what I'm doing. I'm going to sleep."

Aghast, she cried, "But you can't! Not here!"

He half turned and looked over his shoulder at her, his dark hair attractively disheveled. "If you're inviting me to join you in your bed, I won't say no."

She refused to dignify that remark with an answer. "I'm calling my attorney, Kon."

"It's awfully late, isn't it? But you can try," he said in a bored voice. Then he lay back down and punched the bolster a couple of times to get into a more comfortable position.

Meg whirled around and dashed into the kitchen.

The receiver was missing. He must have detached and hidden it while she was putting Anna back to bed.

"Relax. You're perfectly safe with me here. If by morning you still want to call your attorney, go ahead. All it means is that you'll end up meeting Senator Strickland sooner rather than later. Sweet dreams, Meggie."

She made a noise that sounded like something between a cry and a groan, impotently staring at Kon's back. Within minutes, she heard his breathing change. He'd actually fallen asleep!

What was she going to do? Kidnap Anna from her own apartment?

A mirthless laugh escaped. Short of rendering her daughter unconscious, she'd never manage. Anna wouldn't stand to be dragged away from Kon when they'd only just been united. And where could Meg take her without being followed?

Physically and emotionally drained, she reflected on comments one of her divorced friends at work had made. Cheryl had talked about how hard it was dealing with an ex-husband who still acted as if he was part of the family. She'd described her feelings of oppression and claustrophobia, and her frequent sense of fear.

For the first time Meg thought she understood a little of what Cheryl had meant. But Meg suspected that if she was to tell her friend about her past association with Kon, about what had happened to her and Anna during the ballet, the other woman wouldn't believe her. Meg could hardly believe it herself.

Yet one of her deepest fears had already been realized. Kon had taken Anna's heart by storm. As for Meg's other fear—that he would insist on taking Anna to live with him for part of the year—only time would reveal Kon's true intentions.

Instead of being relieved by the insight he'd provided about his forced recruitment to the KGB at such a tender age, Meg found that it only deepened her anxiety. After all, Kon had been brutally torn from his own family, with everyone lost to him. Then he'd learned of Anna's existence. What could be more natural than to claim his own flesh and blood to fill that void?

Today's episode at the ballet provided Meg with absolute proof that from now on, wherever he went, whatever he did, he'd make sure his adoring daughter was by his side. And he'd let no one stand in the way, least of all Meg.

Kon was an expert at manipulation and intrigue. What would be the point of contacting her attorney or Senator Strickland, or the CIA for that matter? None of them was capable of giving her the reassurance she needed.

This was a crisis without precedent, one she'd have to work through by herself. Kon's first step would be to lull her into a false sense of security—then he'd strike. Eventually they'd have to battle it out in court.

Perhaps the best thing for now would be to play along until she saw her way clear to thwart him.

A shiver passed through her body. She turned off the Christmas-tree lights, and Kon was no longer visible. But somehow the darkness tended to magnify his presence.

The irony of the situation wasn't lost on Meg. At one time she would have given everything she possessed to see him lying there on her couch. After learning she was pregnant, her ultimate fantasy had been to see Kon walk through the front door straight into her arms.

I was out of my mind, she berated herself, wishing with all her soul that she'd had the wisdom to listen to her aunt.

After Meg had lost both parents, she'd lived with her aunt, Margaret, who'd been crippled with arthritis and suffered from a bad heart. Margaret had been horrified when Meg finally found the courage to tell her about the incident in Moscow, which had resulted in her being arrested and jailed.

Margaret was the widow of Meg's uncle Lloyd, her father's brother and a man with a distinguished career in naval intelligence. He'd died tragically from a slip on the ice when Meg was in her early twenties. Lloyd had been the most vocal in questioning the wisdom of Meg's Russian studies, let alone her traveling to the USSR. Margaret had seconded his opinions.

The brothers had had opposing viewpoints about Russia's threat to the world. Meg's father was not only a pacifist but a political scientist who'd believed language was the basis of understanding other people.

He'd argued that there would come a time when the two nations could coexist peacefully. The U.S. would need teachers and ambassadors who understood and spoke Russian, people like Meg.

Uncle Lloyd, on the other hand, had remained adamant that the kind of situation his brother described was a pipe dream. He'd used all the cold hard facts at his command to support his arguments. When Meg told her aunt about the incident, Margaret had reiterated those facts, saying that if Uncle Lloyd had still been alive, he would have made an international incident of his niece's incarceration.

Meg hadn't been able to understand why her aunt was so upset. After all, she'd told her how the attractive KGB agent had intervened and gotten her to the airport in time to make it home for the funeral, how he'd given her a farewell gift.

But the more she defended him, the more her aunt argued. Margaret had finally confided inside information she'd gleaned from her husband about the mission of the KGB, not the sort of thing made public to the American people, details learned from several important Soviet defectors.

When Meg looked back, she felt remorse for having treated her aunt with scorn and disbelief. It seemed that Meg was her father's daughter, and she'd brushed off Margaret's advice, never dreaming that one day the older woman's warnings would come back to haunt her.

About the time Anna was born, Meg's aunt had passed away. Right after that, detente occurred. Stories began to trickle out of Russia about the inner workings of the KGB. To Meg's horror, it appeared that everything her aunt had tried to tell her was true.

And now Kon was here, a new threat to her peace of mind.

Suddenly Meg felt limp with exhaustion. She made her way to the bedroom, where she changed into a loose-fitting T-shirt and sweatpants. Taking the pillow from her bed, she went into Anna's room, needing comfort.

She climbed under the quilt and pulled Anna close, wrapping her arms around her. She caught her breath—the faint scent of Kon's soap lingered on Anna's cheek and hair. With a groan she turned sharply away and smothered her face in the pillow.

The clean fragrance brought back poignant memories of Kon on the last night they were together. She remembered the smoldering blue of his eyes before he made love to her, his insatiable desire for her and the Russian endearments that poured from his soul. Once again, he'd begged her to be his wife, to stay with him forever.

Meg never tired of hearing those words, and she'd told him there was nothing she wanted more—as long as they could arrange to spend half the year in Russia and the other half in the States. Through her uncle's contacts at the Pentagon and Kon's position in his government, surely something could be arranged. Since both of them loved their countries, it seemed the only solution if they were to have a life together.

He'd shaken his head. "What you want is an impossibility, Meggie. The only way we can be together is for you to give up your citizenship and live with me.

You have no family now. If you love me enough, you'll do it.''

"I think you must know how much I love you, Kon. But what if you grow tired of me? I couldn't bear that," she'd whispered into his hair, clinging to him. "What would happen if you decided you didn't want me anymore and asked for a divorce? I'd be alone, unable to return to the States.''

Kon had responded with an anger that was all the more terrible because it was so quiet and controlled. He'd disentangled himself from her body and climbed out of bed to get dressed. Devastated by his reaction, Meg drew the covers to her chin and sat up.

He'd trained accusing eyes on her. "You don't know the meaning of love if you can lie in my arms and talk about marriage and divorce in the same breath. One of the problems in your country—"

"Not just my country, Kon—" she interrupted him, then fell silent. The last magical night they'd shared began to disintegrate.

In a few long strides he was out the bedroom door while she sponge-bathed as best she could, then dressed for the trip to the airport. Kon took her cases to the car and helped her inside, all the while ignoring her questions and overtures. His frozen silence broke her heart.

Once more he was the forbidding and unapproachable KGB agent. He'd rushed her to the airport in record time, instructed a guard to deal with her bags, then walked her to the plane. The way he'd helped her find her seat reminded Meg of the first time she'd left Russia.

Déjà vu except for one thing. She and Kon were alone inside the huge body of the jet. No other passengers had been allowed to board yet. Meg felt torn, and she wondered if a human being could endure this much pain and still survive.

"Meggie..."

She remembered the tortured sound of his voice and how she'd let out a gasp and looked at him. Perhaps it was the shadowy interior that had made his eyes glisten.

"Don't go. Stay with me. I love you, *mayah labof*. We'll be married right away. I have plenty of money. You can have your choice of the finest apartments. We'll live very well. I'll always take care of you," he'd vowed in an almost savage voice before crushing her in his arms.

More than anything in the world, she'd wanted to say yes. She'd molded herself to him, kissing him with all the intensity that was in her. But she was too much a product of her Western upbringing. Fear of what might happen in the future kept her from accepting his proposal.

Consumed by tears and frantic because their time had run out, she'd cried, "Do you think I want to leave you? My life is never going to be the same without you!"

At her words an expressionless mask had come down over his face and he'd held her at a distance.

"Kon, don't look at me like that! I can't bear it. I-I'll save my money and try to come back next year."

"No." He'd ground the word out with a strange finality she didn't understand. "Don't come back. Do you hear me?'' He shook her hard. ''Don't ever come back.''

''But—''

''It's now or not at all.''

His implacability had defeated her and she'd slumped against him, sobbing. ''With you, I'm not afraid. But if something happened to you, I'd have nowhere to turn.''

She heard his sharp intake of breath. ''Goodbye, Meggie.'' He'd let her go and started down the aisle. Any second, and he would disappear from her life forever.

She'd cried his name in panic, but it was like shouting into the wind.

He was gone.

CHAPTER FIVE

"MOMMY! MOMMY!" Meg felt a pat on her face. "Why are you crying?"

Meg awoke from her half sleep with a start and stared at her daughter through bleary eyes, completely disoriented. *It was morning.* "I—I must have had a bad dream."

"Is that why you slept with me?"

After a brief hesitation Meg said, "Yes."

"You should have slept with Daddy. Then you wouldn't have been scared. Melanie says her mommy and daddy sleep together except when they have fights. Then he sleeps at her grandma's. Did you and Daddy have a fight?"

Was there any subject of a delicate nature Anna and Melanie *hadn't* discussed?

Meg expelled an exasperated sigh and threw back the covers to get out of bed, deciding not to comment. Anna must have been up for some time because she'd dressed in her favorite blue velour top with the pink hearts and matching pants. And Meg hadn't even been aware of it.

Anxiety made her reach out and cling to her daughter for an extra-long moment. Anna hugged her back, then struggled to be free.

"We had pancakes for our breakfast but I told him you like toast so he fixed that and said I should come and get you."

Now that Anna mentioned it, Meg could smell coffee. Since Anna didn't know how to prepare coffee, that meant Kon had taken over. As he always did, commandeering the apartment, her daughter, her life—

But could she really expect him to act in any other way, know any other method—an eight-year-old boy stolen by the state and taught to be the complete authority figure?

Furious to find herself thinking of *any* excuse for him, Meg vented her feelings on the bed, which she'd started to make. Anything to put off the moment she had to face him again.

"Hurry, Mommy. I want to go see our house and the dogs."

"But we'll miss your Sunday-school class," Meg reminded her, already knowing how Anna would react. She couldn't help saying it, anyway.

"Daddy says there's a church by our house. I can go to Sunday school there next week. He says there are six kids in my class."

Meg's movements became so jerky she actually ripped the top sheet, which had caught on the end of the metal frame.

Anna's eyes rounded. "Uh-oh, Mommy. Something tore."

"So it did," Meg mumbled and threw on the comforter before she headed to the bathroom.

"I'll tell Daddy you're up!"

After Anna darted off, Meg glanced at herself in the mirror. A pale, haggard face stared back, but that was just fine with her. She took care of the necessities, then pulled her hair back, securing it with an elastic. She decided against makeup or perfume. For that matter, she'd leave on her sweats. The vivacious young woman who used to do everything possible to make herself beautiful for Kon had died.

"Mommy? Telephone!"

Meg's head jerked sideways. She hadn't even heard it ring. Kon must have reattached the receiver earlier that morning and picked it up the instant it rang.

"Coming."

She hated it that the second she saw Kon standing by the wall with the receiver in one hand, a cup of coffee in the other, her heart thumped crazily in her chest. She avoided his disquieting gaze as she took the phone from him, then turned her back. It should be a sin for a man to be so attractive that her senses couldn't help responding to him. Even her palms had moistened.

"Hello?" She strove to sound calm and normal.

"Am I speaking to Ms. Meg Roberts?"

Meg blinked at the sound of an officious-sounding female voice.

"Yes?"

"Please stay on the line. Senator Strickland would like to speak to you."

She leaned against the doorjamb for support and concentrated on Anna. At Kon's urging the child began to clean up the mess she'd made on the table with her nail polish. She'd obviously been getting ready for their trip.

"Ms. Roberts? Senator Strickland."

She instantly recognized that aging, raspy voice with the sustained pauses. "Yes, Senator."

"I'm calling to offer you my support and assure you that I couldn't be happier about the reunion with that young man of yours."

Reunion? Young man?

"I'd say that any man who would go through this kind of pain, danger and suffering must truly be in love. You realize your young man was one of the Soviets' most important defectors? And then there were the six years of semi-isolation while he waited to claim his American sweetheart and child.... I understand you're having some difficulty with the situation. But Mr. Rudenko deserves a hearing and I damn well hope you're giving him one."

Meg surmised that the two CIA agents had already filled him in on last night's meeting with her and he wasn't happy about it. But she was incapable of making more than a noncommittal sound in reply.

"My wife and I would consider it an honor if you would plan to join us for dinner soon. I'll have my secretary arrange it with you after the Christmas holidays. You two need time alone to renew the romance and make plans. I envy you that." He chuckled amicably.

Meg felt she was going to suffocate. "Th-thank you, Senator," she whispered.

"If there's anything I can do for you in the meantime, you call my secretary and she'll let me know. I'm sure this will be a very merry Christmas."

The line went dead. In a daze she put the phone back on the hook only to hear it ring again. She could feel Kon's penetrating gaze as she lifted the receiver once more. Clearing her throat she said, "Hello?"

"Hi."

Her eyes closed tightly. "Hi, Ted."

"Hey? What's wrong? You don't sound like yourself."

She rubbed the back of her neck with her free hand and walked as far into the living room as the cord would allow, away from prying eyes and ears.

"I—I guess I've come down with something." Even if Kon hadn't turned her world inside out, she still would have proffered an excuse not to go out with Ted. She didn't mind lunch with him once in a while, but that was it. He didn't interest her. No man did.

"I'm sorry to hear that. I was about to ask if you and Anna wanted to go sledding with me at the park this afternoon. Afterward I figured we'd get dinner someplace."

Now he was trying to appeal to her by including Anna. "That sounds very nice. Maybe another time when I'm feeling better," she lied.

"Right." The disappointment in his voice was palpable. "Then I'll see you at the office."

"Yes. I should be there tomorrow. I'm sure all I need is a good night's sleep. Thanks for calling."

Aware she sounded nervous, she said goodbye, dreading the short walk to the kitchen to hang up the phone.

"Ted Jenkins, salesman of the year at Strong Motors," Kon said, clearly baiting her. "Thirty years old. Divorced. Frustrated because he doesn't have a relationship with you and never will. Why don't you eat your breakfast while I help Anna on with her snowsuit? Then we can be off."

"How do you know about him?"

"Like any man in love, I made it my business to find out if I had serious competition. Walter Bowman was willing to go in there on the pretext of buying a sports car. Ted Jenkins ended up taking him for a test run, and by the end of the ride, he'd learned enough to give me the information I wanted."

Under normal circumstances, any woman would be thrilled to know that the man she loved cared that much. But nothing about their relationship was normal.

Still, part of her *was* thrilled. And that meant it was starting to happen all over again.... Ignoring the plate of cold toast sitting on the counter, Meg fled from the room. She felt a desperate need to avoid Kon's probing gaze.

He didn't play fair! And she was terrified he would discover the kind of power he still had over her. The wisest thing would be to pretend to go along with his plan for Anna's sake.

Their daughter was determined to see where he lived. Once her curiosity had been satisfied, Meg would tell Kon he'd have to work through her attorney if he hoped to spend time with Anna after today. Any future visits would have to be in Meg's presence.

No matter that he'd somehow gained the confidence of Senator Strickland, Kon wasn't above the law. Her anger made her motions clumsy and she broke a shoelace. She groaned in frustration. Now she'd have to wear loafers instead of running shoes.

"Here's your coat, Mommy. Daddy's outside warming up the car for us."

"Well, wasn't that thoughtful of him," she muttered sarcastically beneath her breath. She was bristling with indignation at the thought that he'd taken her keys off the counter without even asking.

"Daddy says you need a rest, so he's going to drive. He says you've been working too hard, so he's going to take good care of you."

Meg couldn't let this go on any longer. After buttoning her coat, she crouched down to talk to her daughter, who was clutching her doll. "Honey—" she smoothed the dark curls, which bounced right back over Anna's forehead "—I know you're happy about meeting your daddy, but that doesn't mean we're all going to live together."

"Yes, it does," Anna said with complete assurance. "I told Daddy I wanted a baby sister like Melanie's. And you know what?" Her eyes grew rounder. "He said he could give me a sister just as soon as you get married next week. He wants a big family."

Meg gasped out loud and buried her face against Anna's small shoulder. "Anna! Mommy isn't going to marry your daddy."

"Yes, you are," she stated confidently. "Daddy said so. He promised he's going to stay home with us all the time. Don't be scared, Mommy." She stroked Meg's hair.

Meg clung to her daughter for a full minute before getting control of herself. "Sometimes grown-ups can't keep their promises, Anna."

"Daddy will 'cause he's my daddy and he loves me," she argued, sounding close to tears. "Let's hurry, Mommy. He's waiting for us."

She broke free of Meg's grasp and scuttled out of the apartment before Meg could stop her. Afraid of what was already happening to Anna, Meg grabbed her purse from the kitchen counter, locked the door and dashed after her.

Luckily, Sunday mornings were quiet around the complex, especially during the winter. Most of her neighbors were still inside their apartment, and Meg was spared answering difficult questions like, *Why do you look so pale, Meg? Who's the attractive stranger who stayed over at your apartment last night? Why is he driving your Toyota with Anna seated up front next to him?*

Kon got out of the car at her approach, his eyes narrowed on her face. More than ever, she was glad she hadn't dressed up or bothered with makeup. Most likely he was comparing the tired, anxiety-ridden mother to the passionate, love-besotted young woman she used to be.

"If you'd rather drive, I'll sit in back," he offered.

He sounded so reasonable her temper flared. "Why break your record and give me a choice now?" She kept on walking around the other side of the car and climbed into the back before he could help her.

He followed her and shut the door. After a searching glance, which she refused to meet, he went around to the driver's side and got in. Seconds later, they were off.

He turned on a radio station playing Christmas carols and Anna began singing, much to Kon's delight. Meg could see his face through the rearview mirror as he sang with her. She couldn't help but be touched by the adoring expression he cast Anna every so often.

As the Toyota covered the miles, it dawned on Meg that she'd never been chauffeured around in her own car before. It was a novel experience to ride in the back seat and let Kon do the work, all the while keeping their loquacious daughter entertained. Grudgingly Meg admitted that not having to be in charge made a nice change, especially now, with the roads growing icy and wind buffeting the car.

But of course if Kon wasn't in the picture, she would never have gone driving with Anna on a wintry day like today in the first place. Their normal routine was to walk to the church a few blocks away, then come home and fix lunch. Afterward, Meg usually encouraged Anna to practice her violin. Then her daughter would either play at Melanie's apartment, or vice versa, while Meg caught up on some reading or sewing.

Lately Anna had been spending more time at Melanie's because of her fascination with the new baby. This was why she'd become so obsessed with the idea of having a brother or sister of her own and had divulged her fantasies to Kon. So far he'd proved he could grant her every desire. Was it any wonder that Anna adored him? Just the way *Meg* had once adored him?

Unable to help herself, she found her eyes straying to the back of his dark head, the broad set of his shoulders, his incredibly handsome profile. *There ought to be a law!* she cried inside. Abruptly she turned away to stare out the window, but not before his smoldering glance had intercepted hers for an instant. It sent a shock wave through her body, disrupting the rhythm of her breathing.

The force of her own reaction upset her so much she didn't realize that they'd pulled into a rest area and come to a stop.

"I don't have to go to the bathroom yet, Daddy."

Despite Kon's low chuckle, Meg felt nervous, wondering why they'd stopped. He turned in the seat so he could eye both of them.

"We're almost at Hannibal. But before we get there, I have a secret to tell you." His grave tone increased Meg's apprehension. "I know your mother can keep it, but what about you, Anochka? If I tell you something very, very important, will you remember that it is our family secret, no one else's?"

Our family. Meg's breath caught while Anna's eyes grew solemn and she slowly nodded her head.

"When I left Russia, I had to change my name."

"Why, Daddy?"

Meg felt a strange tension radiating from him, as if there was a surfeit of dark emotion he had difficulty suppressing.

"Some people got mad because I left my country," he said in a hollow voice, "and some people in America were mad because I came here. They didn't like my Russian name. They didn't like me."

Something in his tone led Meg to believe he'd suffered. Anna was equally affected.

"We like you, Daddy!" She rushed to her father's defense, her child's heart ready to forgive him anything. "We *love* you, don't we, Mommy?"

"And I love both of you," he said in a husky voice, preventing Meg from refuting him. "So to keep us all safe, I took a different name."

With such important news to consider, Anna forgot to sing along with the carol that had just started playing on the radio, even though "Deck the Halls" was one of her favorites. "What's your new name?"

"Gary Johnson."

Gary Johnson? Meg fought to keep from bursting out laughing. No man in the world ever looked or acted less like a Gary Johnson than KGB agent Konstantin Rudenko. It was ludicrous.

"That's the name of a boy in my class!" Anna cried excitedly. "He's got blond hair and a pet c-coca-too. Mrs. Beezley let us bring our pets to class and Mommy helped me bring my fish."

Kon nodded, seemingly pleased with her response. "Thousands of boys and men in the United States have the name Gary Johnson. That's why I picked it."

"And now nobody's mad at you anymore?"

"That's right. I have lots of new friends and neighbors, and they all call me Gary or Mr. Johnson."

"Can't I keep calling you Daddy?"

Kon undid her seat belt and pulled her onto his lap so he could kiss her. "You're the only person in the whole wide world who gets to call me Daddy, Anochka."

"'Cept when I get a new sister."

"That's right," he murmured, hugging her tight.

Anna finally lifted her head so she could see over the seat, her blue eyes glowing like jewels. "Mommy, you have to call Daddy Gary from now on. Don't forget," she said in a hushed voice.

Anna's remark was so touching, Meg's heart turned over and she averted her eyes. As far as Kon went, though, it would be impossibile for her to call him Gary. In fact, the whole situation was too fantastic: she just couldn't do it. But that really didn't matter, because she wouldn't be seeing him except at visitation times, and then they wouldn't be around other people.

She felt Kon's glance sweep over her. "Your mommy has always called me 'darling,' so I don't anticipate any problem."

Meg couldn't take much more of this farce. She felt as though she'd aged a hundred years since the ballet yesterday.

"I think another snowstorm's coming, *Gary*," she mocked. "If we're going to see your house, then I suggest we get moving."

His brilliant smile twisted her insides. "It sounds as if you're as excited as I am."

After he'd put Anna back in her seat and fastened the belt, he started the car and they reentered the freeway. Hannibal was only six miles farther. "I can hardly wait until we get home," he confided to his daughter, tousling her curls with his free hand. "I've been lonely for my little girl."

"I'm here now, Daddy, and you won't ever be lonely again, will he, Clara?" she said to the doll she'd named after the girl in the *Nutcracker*. "Clara loves you, too, Daddy."

"I'm glad to hear it."

Hard as she tried, Meg couldn't blot out the sound of his deep, attractive voice or the loving look he exchanged with their daughter. Anna's sweet, generous spirit brought a lump to Meg's throat, and it seemed to have affected Kon in a similar manner, because he whispered the Russian word for sweetheart and reached for Anna's hand.

The takeover was complete. Anna would never be wholly hers again. Meg couldn't bear it and she put a hand over her heart, as if she could stop the pain. *What was she going to do?*

They left the freeway and entered the small town of Hannibal, made famous by Sam Clemens, who had written about his boyhood on the Mississippi in the mid-nineteenth century.

Meg didn't know what Kon had in mind, but supposed that for Anna's sake he would drive them past the riverboat landing in the downtown area, where the Mark Twain Home and Museum were located.

Instead, he took a route that led past all the historic homes decorated for Christmas until they came to the famous Rockcliffe Mansion. They drove another block, then he turned a corner and entered a driveway that needed to be shoveled after last night's snow. They wound around the back of a quaint, white, two-story clapboard house with green trim; it reminded her of the restored Becky Thatcher Bookshop in the historic district.

"We're home, Anochka." He pulled to a stop in front of a detached two-car garage and undid Anna's seat belt.

Anna couldn't keep still, her bright eyes missing nothing. "Where are my dogs, Daddy?"

"On the back porch, waiting for us."

Meg stared at the house in disbelief, then switched her gaze to Kon. He was helping Anna from the car, her doll forgotten. Meg couldn't equate this doting father and family man with the all-powerful KGB agent who, at one time, had inspired fear in the hearts of Soviet citizens and foreigners alike.

She got out of the car, then watched spellbound as Kon told both of them to wait right there while he mounted the steps and unlocked the door.

Anna let out a shriek of delight as a handsome German shepherd came running down the stairs and circled her in the snow, sniffing at her hands and swishing his tail. No doubt Kon had experience with dogs trained in pursuit. This one had been handled so expertly he didn't bare his teeth or growl or jump up on her, relieving Meg of any initial worry in that department.

At Kon's command, the dog came to a standstill and let Anna pet him. It didn't surprise Meg that her daughter showed no fear. An elderly couple across the street from the apartment complex had a friendly golden retriever Anna and Melanie loved to play with.

"Meggie, come over and meet Thor," Kon urged, his voice alive and inviting. It conjured up memories of another place, another time, when she'd lived for nothing but him and whenever they were apart counted the hours till they were together again.

For the next few minutes Meg let go of her anxieties about Kon's motives long enough to become acquainted with the dog. Thor appeared as ecstatic as Anna to make friends. He showed his affection with licks and whimpers and a few exuberant barks that made Anna giggle and her father laugh out loud.

Meg had never heard such a happy sound from him. Forgetting to be on her guard, she raised her head, smiling, and discovered he was looking at her in the old way, his eyes fiercely blue and possessive. She felt her body tremble and turned away.

"Where's the other dog?" Anna wanted to know.

"Gandy's busy inside," came the cryptic reply. "Shall we go see what she is doing?"

"Follow me, Thor," Anna cried excitedly as she scrambled up the back steps behind her father. Before Meg had even reached the door she heard Anna's awestruck voice. Curious to see what had produced such reverence, Meg hurried into the warm, closed-in porch, where she caught a glimpse of a female German shepherd lying on a makeshift bed in the corner, with three tiny suckling pups. The new mother lifted her proud head at their approach.

Thor crept next to Kon, who hunkered down and put his arm around Anna while they gazed at the beautiful sight. "This is the early Christmas present I told you about, Anochka," he whispered.

"Oh, Daddy!" she squealed in rapture. "Look at the littlest one. She could fit in my hands."

"She's a he." His voice was tender, gently mocking.

Anna absorbed that bit of information and said, "Can I hold him? Please?"

"In a little while, when he's through eating. We musn't disturb them right now."

"What's his name?" she whispered loudly. With Anna, there was no such thing as a quiet whisper.

"I thought I'd leave that up to you since he'll be your dog. The other two we'll find a new home for as soon as they're ready to leave their mommy. But this puppy's just for you."

Once again Anna's eyes looked like exploding stars as she turned to Meg. "Mommy, I'm going to call him Prince Marzipan Johnson."

Meg started to laugh—she couldn't help it—and Kon joined her.

"Why don't we call him Prince for short?" Kon finally managed to say. He got to his feet. "I think we've tried Gandy's patience long enough. Why don't you go inside with Thor and start exploring." He opened another door that led into the house. "See if you can pick out your bedroom."

"*My own bedroom?* Come on, Thor." She put a hand on the dog's collar and they squeezed through the opening together. Meg couldn't tell which one of them was the most excited. But the moment they disappeared, the reality of the situation pressed in on Meg until she could hardly breathe.

"Kon—"

"Later, Meggie. Unless you want to join me in the shower."

She jammed her hands in her coat pockets and fastened her attention on Gandy, who'd returned her attention to the pups. Long after Kon had gone into the house, Meg stood there, willing the image of his hard, fit body, which had once known and claimed hers, to leave her mind.

The bittersweet torture of those memories held her unmoving, and though Anna was calling her, Meg couldn't bring herself to step one foot inside Kon's house. A house she suspected he'd bought with money he'd been paid for selling secrets.

CHAPTER SIX

MEG WAS AFRAID.

Afraid she'd like his home too much. Afraid he'd break down her resolve a little more, until the edges blurred and she didn't know what was phony and what was real. Afraid she'd be like Anna, totally vulnerable and accepting, until—until what? Meg didn't know anymore.

Even if he *had* defected, he was still a son of Russia, a man who loved his country. Now that a detente had been reached, she wouldn't blame him for wanting to return to his birthplace, that isolated village in Siberia for a visit. A place where he'd played with his sled as a little boy, where he'd been happy in the bosom of his family.

He had money and he could travel under an American passport. And he could take Anna with him. What could be more natural than to want to recapture his own stunted childhood through his daughter's eyes, to instill in her his love of Mother Russia? If he had joint custody, he could take Anna wherever he wanted and Meg would never need to know.

Ages ago, she'd turned down his marriage proposal because she hadn't wanted to live in Russia on a permanent basis. That would never change. Kon knew how she felt. She was sure there'd be no warning if he uprooted Anna temporarily.

It was time to have a talk with him.

An excess of nervous energy propelled her into the house. But halfway through the kitchen Meg came to a halt, arrested by the white ceiling-to-counter cabinets in the traditional British pantry style. Wide cherry floorboards gleamed with a golden patina against white moldings and pale yellow walls, creating a sense of mellow warmth and beauty. It was a classic look that was continued throughout the rest of the downstairs.

The moderately sized house with its old-fashioned, small-paned windows reflected a spare traditionalism. The use of a few period pieces in the living and dining rooms, combined with comfortable, overstuffed furniture covered in a predominantly green chintz, gave it a timeless appeal.

Her eye followed the graceful sweep of the staircase with its hand-carved railing. Slowly she wandered into a study set off by French doors. Two pilastered bookcases on either side of a brick fireplace contained an impressive library of classical literature, with books in several languages, including, of course, Russian.

File cabinets and a desk complete with lamp, computer, keyboard and monitor supplied the only modern touch.

Did the decor reflect Kon's personal taste or had he purchased this charming home as is?

How could she possibly know the real man beneath his KGB-created persona when her only contact with him had been inside a police car, or a hotel or restaurant staffed by KGB?

Or a woodcutter's cottage?

Meg shivered as she contemplated the enormity of what she'd done. Anna had been conceived in a stranger's bed, by a stranger, in a strange land....

Certainly Kon couldn't have taken his lover home with him in those days, wherever and whatever "home" might have been. The normal human experience of a man and woman meeting and getting to know each other had eluded her completely where he was concerned.

According to Walt and Lacey Bowman, Kon had lived here in Hannibal for five years. Had the American government provided him with this house, along with a ready-made identity to hide the fact that he was a Russian defector?

Who was the real Kon?

Was Konstantin Rudenko the name his parents had given him at birth, or had the Soviet government supplied him a new one when they'd kidnapped him for service?

Meg thought she'd go mad trying to answer those questions, and she buried her face in her hands.

Another pair of hands settled on her shoulders. Strong, warm, masculine hands that felt achingly familiar. She should have tried to move away, but her body was being controlled by a force more powerful than her will to fight it. A low, husky voice whispered, "Don't try to solve all the world's riddles right now." It was as though he'd read her mind.

Her breath caught as she felt questing fingers encircle the nape of her neck and gently massage the tense muscles. "You and I haven't had a moment alone until now," he murmured, grazing her earlobe with his teeth. "Much as I adore Anna, I thought I'd lose my mind if she didn't find a way to entertain herself so I could kiss her mother. Dear God, it's been six endless, excruciating years, *mayah labof.*"

The heat from his body radiated to Meg's, and those old, familiar longings took over, trapping her despite everything she knew and feared about him. His mouth traveled along her hot cheek, his smooth, freshly shaved skin scented from the soap he'd used in the shower.

"There's been no one else for me since you left me, and I have the strongest impression there's been no one else for you, either. What we shared could never be repeated with anyone else. Help me," he groaned against her lips before drawing her fully into his arms.

Meg tried not to respond, but she felt as if some drug had dulled her power to think, to remember that he was the enemy. His mouth started to work its magic, and before she knew how it had happened, her mouth opened to his. Her passion flared out of control. Just like before...

It was happening again, just as she'd feared. The mindless rapture, this explosion of sensual feeling that left her weak and clinging to him. It had been so long since the last time he'd aroused these sensations that her desire leapt to pulsating life.

Somehow, without her being aware of it, he'd undone her coat and now he was urging her body closer, running his hands over her back, insinuating his fingers beneath the waistband of her skirt to touch her sensitized skin.

With a helpless moan she slid her arms around his neck, and her body arched against his solid warmth, knowing where this was leading, wanting it so badly, she was barely conscious of footsteps running down the stairs and an excited young voice chatting with Thor.

Anna.

Meg couldn't let her daughter see them like this. She shoved her hands against his chest, but Kon must not have heard Anna, because he deepened their kiss, effectively suffocating her cry of panic.

His mouth craved hers with the relentless hunger of a man who'd been deprived too long. To her shame, Meg offered herself in wanton abandon even as Anna came bouncing into the study with an exuberant Thor at her heels.

Mortified to have been caught out like this, Meg tried to pull away from Kon and waited for the inevitable comment from their curious, precocious daughter. But for once, Anna failed to say anything at all.

The unnatural silence must have alerted Kon, who with a low groan reluctantly lifted his mouth from hers. His eyes burned a hot blue as they studied her trembling mouth.

Since he seemed as incapable of speech as his daughter, Meg realized it was up to her to divert Anna's attention.

She took advantage of Kon's temporary weakness to separate herself from him. But she wasn't prepared for the sense of loss she felt as soon as she'd moved out of his arms. Nor was she prepared for the speculative look in Anna's eyes; it reminded her of Kon—the same penetrating gaze. Thor rubbed against Anna's side, waiting.

Heavens, Anna made Meg feel like a lovestruck teenager whose parents had found her in a compromising position with her boyfriend! Before she could think of something to say to defuse the situation, Anna took the initiative.

"Have you and Daddy been making a baby?"

She should have been ready for that one. Her breathing grew shallow as she felt Kon's hands slide to her shoulders. He kneaded them with gentle insistence.

"Not yet, Anochka," he answered calmly. "First your mother has to agree to marry me. Shall I ask her now?"

"No! Please..." Meg begged him, but Anna was nodding solemnly, and Meg knew she herself would have fainted if Kon hadn't been standing behind her, holding her in his firm grip.

"Meggie." He ignored her plea and murmured into her hair, caressing the top of her head with his chin. "With Senator Strickland's help, special arrangements have been made for us to have a private wedding here at the house on Wednesday. A friend of mine who's a judge on the state's Supreme Court will marry us, and Lacey and Walt will serve as witnesses. The only detail left is for you to say yes."

Yesterday he'd placed the noose around her neck. Now he'd drawn it tight.

"I want us to be a family. Anna shouldn't have to grow up without her father the way I did, and I certainly don't want anyone else raising her. Obviously you don't, either, or you would have married before now."

Which was true, but she'd rather die than admit it to him.

"You can quit your job at Strong Motors and be a full-time mother to Anna. This house needs a mother and father, husband and wife. I didn't even want to put up a Christmas tree or decorations until we could do it together."

There was a long silence while Meg tried to absorb what he was saying.

"Anna," she finally said in a shaky voice, "I need to talk to your father alone. Why don't you and Thor go out on the porch and see how the new puppies are doing? But don't touch them."

"Are you going to marry my daddy?" the child persisted stubbornly.

"Anna," Meg said as sternly as she could, "do as I say, please."

But her daughter refused to mind her, and the hint of tears shimmering in her eyes was almost more than Meg could bear. "I want to live with Daddy. I have a pink room and a bed with a tent over it, and a mirror and a little table and . . . and everything!"

"Anochka . . ." her father warned quietly. That was all it took for their daughter to grab Thor by the collar and leave the room.

How did Kon do that?

Meg wheeled around in exasperation, noting all at once how incredibly attractive he looked in American jeans and a dark turtleneck. She was determined to ignore her own powerful response to him. "I have no intention of marrying you and we certainly don't need to get married for you to see Anna." Her chest heaved as though she was out of breath. "If you'll tell me what days you want to be with her, I'll drive her here and let you spend time together before I take her home again."

"This is your home now," came the implacable response. "I want both of you here every day and every night for the rest of our lives."

"That isn't possible, Kon. But I'm willing to work out a visitation schedule."

"I'm not."

He was impossible! "It's that or nothing, I'm afraid. You've had your reunion with your daughter. Now I'm taking Anna home. Please give me my car keys."

It shocked her when he reached into his pocket and handed them to her without a word, a strange smile on that darkly handsome face.

It shocked her even more that he did nothing to prevent her from leaving the house. He stood on the steps and kept Thor at bay while Meg dragged an hysterical Anna through the snow to the car.

"Daddy! Daddy!" she screamed at the top of her lungs as Kon went back inside and closed the door. Her daughter's cries reminded Meg of the tape he had played for her the night before. They had to be tearing him apart, yet he didn't lift a finger to help her.

Even though that was what Meg wanted, the pain of the whole thing was almost beyond endurance.

"Don't let Mommy take me away, Daddy!" Anna's heartbreaking plea could be heard for miles, Meg was sure, and the tears didn't stop even when she'd driven away.

Meg found it terrifying that no matter how hard she tried to reason with her daughter, no matter how hard she tried to explain that she could see her father again very soon, Anna cried hysterically all the way home.

"I hate you, Mommy," she said in a hoarse voice when they pulled into their parking spot. "Clara hates you, too, and we're never going to love you again."

Anna's face was flushed and she looked feverish. Guilt almost had Meg restarting the car and returning to Hannibal. But she had to remain firm now or everything would be lost.

Damn you, Kon, she muttered under her breath, fighting back scalding tears of pain and frustration. Before now, there'd never been a discordant note between her and her daughter.

Oh, he was good at his job. Good at creating subversion and chaos! The tears would not be halted now.

Damn you for making me want you, Kon—as badly as Anna wants you. Damn. Damn. Damn!

"Meg? It's an office aide calling from Anna's school. Line two."

Meg closed her eyes. Anna was probably sick. She'd refused to eat any food after they'd gotten home from Hannibal yesterday, and this morning she wouldn't touch her breakfast before Meg drove her to school.

"Thanks, Cheryl."

With a trembling hand Meg picked up the receiver and pressed the button, her headache so fierce she didn't know how she was going to make it through the rest of the day. Four aspirin still hadn't done the trick, and now she was starting to feel nauseated. If this kept up, she'd have to go home.

"Yes? This is Meg Roberts."

"Hi. This is Carla Morley. I'm helping out today because Mrs. Hixon is home with the flu. I'm just checking with you to see if it's all right if Anna's father drives her home. Anna didn't feel well when she got to school this morning and had me phone him in Hannibal when we couldn't reach you at lunchtime. He drove here as fast as he could."

How did Anna know his phone number unless he gave it to her when Meg was unaware?

"The problem is, you haven't put Mr. Johnson's name on the emergency card, but he said that was because he was out of the country until recently. But as I explained to him, I can't give him permission to take Anna off school grounds unless you give your consent."

Dear God. "Just keep Anna there. I'll be right over. And thank you for being so conscientious." Meg's voice shook. It was entirely possible that without Carla Morley's intervention, Kon could be halfway back to Hannibal with Anna—who was so upset with Meg right now she would have willingly accompanied him anywhere.

Cheryl flashed Meg a look of concern as she hung up the phone. "Is something wrong with Anna? You're as white as a sheet."

"Sh-she's sick." It was the truth. And there was no way she could tell anyone about Kon right now, not even Cheryl. "I'm going to have to take her home. Would you mind covering for me?"

"Of course not. You shouldn't have come to work this morning, anyway. Go home and stay there until you're both better."

"Thanks, Cheryl. I'll cover for you next time."

On her way out of the car showroom, Ted tried to engage her in conversation, but Meg told him Anna was sick and she couldn't stop to talk. He went out to the back lot with her and helped her into the car, telling her he'd call later to see if there was anything he could do.

Meg thanked him for his concern but told him it wasn't necessary. Then she didn't give him another thought as she drove the seven miles to Anna's school. Fortunately for her, the storm predicted the day before had failed to materialize. The streets were relatively free of snow, and she broke the speed limit getting to her destination. She parked in the school-bus zone to save time and leapt from the car.

With pounding heart she dashed into the main office, where she discovered Anna sitting on Kon's lap, her curly head resting against his chest. The sight of father and daughter never failed to jolt Meg; they looked so *alike*—and so right together.

Kon's enigmatic gaze rested on Meg. Her sigh of relief at finding her daughter safe quickly changed to one of consternation when she saw Anna's flushed face. "Honey, Ms. Morley said you were sick."

"I don't feel good." The small, weak voice sounded odd to Meg's ears. Caught up in a welter of emotions, she ran directly to Anna, who surprisingly offered no resistance when Meg reached for her. There was no more "I hate you, Mommy," to make her feel worse than she already did.

Ms. Morley flashed her a commiserating smile. "There's a bad flu bug going around. Quite a few of the students are out with it this morning."

"That's probably it," Meg murmured indistinctly. Kon had risen to his full, intimidating height and she could feel his eyes on her, challenging her to make a scene in front of the other woman.

"Luckily today's the last day before Christmas vacation," the aide said amiably. "She'll have the whole holiday to recuperate."

Meg couldn't get out of there fast enough. "Thank you, Ms. Morley."

"Think nothing of it. As soon as Mr. Johnson got here, he was able to calm her down. Seeing her daddy made all the difference, didn't it, Anna?" The woman smiled at Anna, then Kon, obviously charmed by him. "Merry Christmas."

Meg silently blessed the woman for not bringing up the authorization issue. No doubt Ms. Morley dealt with many divorced parents throughout the school year and had learned to be discreet.

"Merry Christmas," Anna called back in a voice that sounded much more cheerful than before.

"How did you know your father's telephone number?" Meg asked Anna the minute they were out of the office. She was acutely conscious of Kon at her elbow opening doors for them.

"I told Ms. Morley that Daddy lives in Hannibal and I said his name was Gary Johnson—like he told us. She called him for me."

To Meg's chagrin, Kon sent her a withering glance. "Our daughter is very bright and resourceful," he began in Russian. "If you're not careful, your paranoia is going to alienate her."

His rebuke made Meg feel small and mean. And guilty, of course, because she was always prepared to think the very worst of him. She realized that, ironically enough, the incident verified at least part of his story, which put him at a moral advantage. That call had proved he was in the phone book, that he had been established for some time.

"Can we go home now? I didn't get to hold Prince yesterday and he misses me."

"I'll take care of him for you, Anochka." Kon had spoken before Meg could manage a word. She felt her world disintegrating a little more—Anna no longer considered their apartment home.

Perhaps Kon noticed that the blood had drained from her face. When he opened the passenger door of Meg's car for Anna, he said, "Right now both you and your mother need to get to bed."

Anna stared up at her with concern. "Are you sick, Mommy?"

"No," Meg hastened to reassure her as Kon fastened the seat belt. "I'm just a little tired."

"Is Daddy coming with us?"

"That's up to your mother," he inserted smoothly, throwing the onus on Meg, who continued to be the villain in this cleverly orchestrated piece.

"Don't go away, Daddy!" Anna started to cry again, deep, heaving sobs that poured from her soul and washed her cheeks in tears. Meg felt suddenly, completely, helpless.

She slumped against the car door, all the fight gone out of her. She didn't have the strength to battle Kon and her daughter, too. In a dull voice she said, "Your father can follow us home in his car if he wants."

Like magic Anna's tears subsided.

Meg expected to see a triumphant expression on Kon's face as he walked her around to the driver's side of the car.

But as he opened the door for her, a brief glint of what looked like pain darkened the blue of his eyes. It fragmented her emotions even more because she had to wonder if he could summon emotion like that at will—just for effect.

"I'll be right behind you, Anochka."

"D-do you p-promise?" Anna's halting question ended on something between a cough and a hiccup.

Meg's hands curled tightly around the steering wheel. She didn't recognize her daughter when Anna behaved like this, when she became this anxiety-ridden child who constantly feared her father would disappear from her life. Her normally trusting and vivacious personality had undergone a complete change.

Apparently Kon was not immune to Anna's fragile condition, either; he unexpectly opened the back door and got into the car. "I'll ride with you and pick up my car later."

Before Meg could fathom it, Anna had unfastened her seat belt and climbed into the back with Kon, flinging her arms around his neck. Meg could see them through the rearview mirror, and her heart seemed to expand with something that felt like pain as she watched the tender way Kon was comforting their daughter. He rocked her back and forth in his strong arms, whispering endearments.

And that was when it came to her. He *loved* Anna.

Emotion like that *couldn't* be faked. Some sixth sense told her that in his own way he adored his little Anochka as much as Meg did. And Anna loved him back just as fiercely. If Meg had held on to the vain hope that this was a passing phase from which Anna would recover once Kon was out of sight, she'd better let go of it now.

The drive back to the apartment was silent, with Meg deep in her own thoughts. When she pulled into her parking spot and got out of the car, she saw that Anna had fallen asleep with her tearstained face half-buried in Kon's neck. The night before, Anna had cried for hours before she'd passed out from exhaustion.

He maneuvered himself and Anna from the back seat without disturbing her and followed Meg into the building.

There were few people around this time of day, for which Meg was thankful. She opened the door of the apartment, and Kon carried Anna to her bedroom. Meg trailed behind them and stood in the doorway, watching the deft way he discarded Anna's parka and shoes and tucked her into bed. He lightly caressed her cheek with the knuckles of one hand. Then abruptly, he straightened and started toward Meg, his expression inscrutable.

A little frightened of the tension between them, she hurried into the living room, feeling far too susceptible to his presence. She wondered if she was on the verge of an emotional breakdown.

"We can be married the day after tomorrow and never have a recurrence of what happened today. But if you're too selfish to think of Anna's best interests, then be warned that I do intend to have a relationship with her."

"What about *my* best interests?" She jerked around, her ash-blond hair and pleated black wool skirt swinging.

He studied her features, the hectic color in her cheeks, her glittering gray eyes, the curves beneath her oyster-colored silk blouse. "You're not in love with anyone else."

"That's beside the point," she lashed out.

"It *is* the point, Meggie. If you'd stayed in Russia, we'd be married today and Anna could easily have a sister or brother by now."

"You're talking about a period of time that's come and gone. I was a totally different human being then! We couldn't possibly have worked anything out because you were already married—to your country. And . . . and I was afraid." Her breath quickened with the force of her emotions.

"I defected," came the swift rejoinder. "Surely that should tell you something."

"Why?" she cried. "*Why* did you defect? It doesn't make sense for a man in your position. And please don't insult my intelligence by telling me you were overcome with love for me!"

His dark brows furrowed. "I may have been a government agent, but I'm still a man, Meggie. One, moreover, who became enamored of a young American woman to the point that I took many dangerous chances, many risks, to spend time with you. When you left, I . . . contracted a disease."

CHAPTER SEVEN

A DISEASE?

Meg's anxious gaze darted to his. "D-did you become ill?" she whispered, her hand going to her throat, where she was positive he could see the hammering of her pulse.

He shifted his weight. "It's a term used by agents to refer to burnout. I'd never had a sick day in my life, and suddenly I went into a depression that left me emotionally ill for months. I lost weight, suffered from insomnia and battled a restlessness I'd never known before.

"As I once told you, there'd been a few other women in the past, mostly other agents working on assignments under me. One relationship lasted a little longer than the rest, but I was always able to move on without becoming emotionally involved."

She hadn't known about the relationship that had gone on longer. How *much* longer? Had he asked that woman to marry him, too? A shaft of pure, unadulterated jealousy left her feeling weak and vulnerable. Until he added, "For some inexplicable reason, it wasn't that easy to walk away from you.

"A comrade suggested I take a leave of absence and go on vacation. So I went to the Urals to do some climbing and fishing. But what should have been a two-week retreat lasted all of two days, and I returned to my post because this restlessness was eating me alive.

"I plunged into my work with such ferocity even my peers tended to stay away from me. But by then I was diagnosed as suffering from severe clinical depression and, oddly enough, the only pleasure I found in life was to follow your movements—through another agent living in the United States."

Meg rubbed her arms, suddenly chilled to the bone, though in reality the apartment was pleasantly warm.

"On one particularly bleak day, the agent telephoned me to say that the beautiful Meg Roberts was pregnant."

He said nothing further for a long moment, apparently lost in recollection. Then he resumed, speaking in a low, rapid voice.

"No one could have been more surprised than I, because I'd taken precautions against that happening." His eyes narrowed on her mouth. "Since I gave you no opportunity to be with another man while in Russia, and since I had irrefutable proof that you hadn't been with another man after leaving the country, I knew you were pregnant with *my* child."

She bowed her head to avoid the possessiveness in his eyes.

"The knowledge that a baby we'd made together was growing inside you took hold of me. It was as if I were there with you, sharing this miraculous experience, and it brought me out of the wretched blackness that had been engulfing me daily.

"When the agent supplied me with a picture of Anna taken while she was still in the hospital nursery, I almost lost my mind. I couldn't be there to hold her, to inspect her fingers and toes, to kiss her soft skin and watch her nurse at your breast. That was the moment I decided to defect."

"Kon..."

"At that point the government was in turmoil, and detente was looking like a real possibility. The changes reshaping my country made me take a long, hard look at my personal life, at my future. All those years I'd served the KGB and that was the only life I'd known.

"But Anna's birth forced me to ask questions about what I wanted for myself." He paced the floor, then came to an abrupt halt. "Don't be deceived by what I'm telling you, Meggie. Russia will always have a claim on my soul. I've been given the finest education in the world, the best lodgings, exceptional pay, diversion when I needed it. And above all, Russia is my homeland. But I found myself wishing that I *belonged* to someone and that someone belonged to me."

He picked up her family photographs from an end table by the couch and studied them for a while. "I don't even know if my parents and sister are still alive. I know nothing about them. They believe I'm dead because this is what they were told thirty years ago. That part is finished."

He put the pictures back and flicked her an indecipherable glance. "I need my daughter. Being with her for the last two days has already filled part of that void in my life."

She sucked in her breath. "If that's how you felt, why didn't you approach me as soon as you arrived in the States? We could have worked out visitation." When she thought of the years that had already gone by...

"When I got out of Russia, I gave your government classified information. The normal procedure was for me to go into hiding. Eventually I was set up with a new identity.

"Since then, the international picture has changed, and the threat isn't the same anymore. But because I know how certain factions of the old guard still think, how the Party mind still works, and because I wanted to make absolutely certain that you and Anna remained unharmed, I waited until now to approach you."

He eyed her steadily. "It was a risk to stay away so long knowing that at any time you could become involved with another man and get married, providing Anna with a stepfather. But it was a risk I had to take because I knew that one day, one way or another, I'd eventually have a relationship with her—and, I hoped, with you."

He gazed at her, a dark, brooding look on his face. "That day is here," he said quietly. "But the choice is yours—do we work out a visitation system, when Anna's already traumatized by everything that's happened? Or do we get married and give her her rightful father and mother?

"In a world where the traditional family unit seems to be disappearing, we're in a position to give her the stability millions of children are denied. The stability I was denied," he added hoarsely.

Maybe she was a gullible fool, but Meg suddenly had the intense conviction that he'd been speaking the truth. Probably because he was so open about telling her that his bond to Russia would never be broken....

"I won't, you know," he murmured, voicing her fears about kidnapping aloud. "Perhaps marrying me is the only way to erase this irrational idea you have that I'm going to take Anna away."

"But you love Russia. I know you do!"

"Yes, but I can't go back, Meggie. My life is here with you. I earn my living at home and I keep a low profile. As my wife, you won't have to work unless you choose. We'll be together twenty-four hours a day. It's what we both wanted before you left Russia." In a low voice he added, "But whether or not you sleep in my bed will be up to you. How does that sound?"

How *did* it sound?

Terrifying, her heart cried. How could she live in the same house with him, year in and year out, wanting him in all the ways a woman wanted a man, yet always feeling afraid he would miss his country, his old life? He said *now* that he couldn't go back, that it was over, but what if he changed his mind? It was all too easy to see how that might happen.

"It's a little matter called trust, Meggie. A rare quality our daughter seems to have in abundance. Apparently she didn't inherit it from you."

Meg reeled from his bitter words. Ignoring her, he took a few strides to the kitchen and reached for the phone.

"Who are you calling?" Meg asked in confusion.

In even tones he said, "I'm simply phoning for a taxi. I need to be driven to my car. The school called me before I could feed and water the dogs. I need to get back to them."

"But if you're not here when Anna w—"

"As I said," he broke in with that arrogant hauteur left over from his KGB days, "visitation has its flaws when we try to function as parents from two separate households." He started punching the buttons.

When she thought of the state Anna would be in when she found him gone, Meg realized she couldn't go through that kind of emotional turmoil again. In a panic she cried, "Wait!"

A tense silence stretched between them. Kon still held the receiver in his hand. "If you're offering to drive me over to Anna's school, it isn't necessary. She needs the sleep and there's no one to mind her." He finished punching the last two numbers.

Her head reared back. "Damn you! You know that isn't what I meant!"

She watched him hang up the receiver, and even from a distance, she could see the glimmer of satisfaction on his face. She despised him for it.

"From the moment you hijacked us at the ballet, you knew you'd win. It was just a matter of time. An agent never accepts losing."

He frowned. "This isn't about agents or ideologies. This is no game, Meggie. I'm fighting for my life,
for you and Anna. Without you, I have no future."

His voice throbbed with naked emotion, and it tore
her apart. His words rang with undeniable conviction, bypassing logic to speak to her soul, success-
fully destroying the last fragile barrier she'd raised
between them.

"AND SO, BY THE POWER vested in me, I now pronounce you husband and wife, legally and lawfully
wedded from this moment on. What God has joined
together, let no man put asunder. You may now kiss
the bride."

Had it been only two days since she'd agreed to
marry him?

From the time Kon had slipped the solitaire dia-
mond ring and wedding band on Meg's finger, he'd
kept hold of her hand. As the final words of the ceremony were pronounced, his grip tightened posses-
sively.

The soft, pale pink chiffon of her calf-length wedding dress flattered her coloring, but she was positive
Kon could detect every fluttering heartbeat through
the thin material. Meg refrained from looking at him,
fearing that she'd see a gloating look in his eyes, a look
of victory.

In fact, from the time she'd entered Kon's living
room with Anna for the late-afternoon ceremony and
had acknowledged Judge Lundquist and the Bowmans—whom she'd learned were not husband and
wife, having adopted the fictitious name as part of

their cover—she had ignored her husband-to-be. Now she closed her eyes as she turned to him for the ritual kiss.

But when she felt his warm mouth unexpectedly brush the backs of both her hands instead of her lips, her eyes flew open in astonishment. She'd never heard of a groom kissing the bride's hands before and wondered if it could be some kind of Russian wedding custom.

Until he suddenly lifted his dark head and his scorching blue eyes trapped her confused gaze. "Finally!" His triumphant whisper told her he'd been aware of her refusal to look at him until now. Before she could react to his subterfuge, his mouth captured hers and he took full advantage, deepening their kiss, demanding a response that stirred her senses in spite of her attempt to remain unmoved.

"It's time for my kiss, Daddy," Anna demanded, pulling at his sleeve. The others chuckled quietly.

Meg was shocked back to reality for an instant when Kon broke their kiss. He scooped Anna from the floor and embraced them both, first kissing his daughter's cheeks, then returning to Meg's unsuspecting mouth, which he kissed so thoroughly she was in danger of forgetting there were other people in the room. Not only that, it seemed Walter Bowman had been filming the proceedings with a camcorder, a revelation that made her flush with embarrassment.

The ringing of the telephone, followed by Lacey Bowman's announcement that Senator Strickland was calling to congratulate them, brought Meg's senses under some semblance of control. She pulled away from Kon on unsteady legs, then bowed her head for a moment, ostensibly to rearrange Anna's crushed nosegay, but actually to take a few steadying breaths. After that, she straightened the collar of her daughter's taffeta dress. Finally she followed Kon into the study to speak to the senator.

The older man did most of the talking, which was just as well, because Meg was so bemused by her new status as Kon's wife she couldn't talk with any coherence. Especially not when Kon's arm slipped around her waist and he held her pressed against his side as if she belonged there.

Anna's voice calling them gave her the excuse to break away from Kon's grip while he finished the conversation with the senator. He seemed reluctant to release her, though, and she felt his gaze on her retreating back as she escaped.

"What is it, honey?" she asked as she hurried into the living room, trying to steady her breathing.

"Look!" Anna squealed happily. "It's Prince Marzipan!"

At first Meg thought she was talking about the puppy. Then her attention was drawn to a large nutcracker—almost two feet high—that her daughter had lifted from a box sitting on the coffee table, the red and green wrapping paper in shambles.

"An early Christmas present from Walt and me," Lacey Bowman murmured in an aside. "Since she loved the ballet, we thought she might like one as a memento."

"See, Mommy?" Anna rushed over to show it to Meg, her face glowing with joy. "He looks like

Daddy! And his mouth opens and closes! Watch!"
She took hold of the handle and worked the jaw of the
beautifully hand-crafted nutcracker. Meg suspected it
had been carved and painted in Russia, rather than
Germany. The detailing of the soldier's cossack hat
and uniform was unmistakable.

By now Kon had reentered the living room and
come to stand behind his daughter, placing his hands
on her shoulders. When Meg sensed his nearness, she
raised her head and gasped softly at the similarity between the dark hair and blue eyes of the toy soldier
and Kon's own striking coloring. The contrast of his
olive complexion against the midnight blue suit and
white shirt was almost dazzling.

He stood tall like the nutcracker, the personifica-
tion of a dark and dashing Russian prince. Meg's
heart took up its crazy thumping and she could easily
imagine him in a cossack uniform and sable hat, a
handsome, impossibly romantic male figure astride his
horse.

Her husband.

She swallowed hard and turned a flushed face to the
judge, who winked at her, then proposed a toast to the
happy family. Meg drank the champagne Lacey served
each of them. Kon declined his drink to pick up
Anna—nosegay, nutcracker and all. Teasingly, he
helped her to a champagne glass of cranberry juice so
she could feel part of the celebration.

Despite Meg's attempt to harden her heart against
Kon, his devotion to their daughter pierced her armor. She couldn't deny that, though Anna had always been a happy child, Kon's appearance in their

lives had added another dimension of loving; even in
the short time that had elapsed, his presence had
boosted Anna's confidence and made her feel that
much more secure.

On Monday evening, when she'd awakened from a
much-needed sleep to learn that her mommy had decided to marry her daddy after all, Anna's almost
hysterical reaction to everything Meg did or didn't do
immediately disappeared.

Instead, an inner glow seemed to radiate from her,
and she was at peace again. She cooperated willingly
with all the packing and work involved in moving an
entire household to a new town. Meg noticed that their
impending marriage had produced such a calming effect on Anna the difference in her behavior was like
night and day.

Everyone at the wedding could see how delighted
she was with her daddy, and Walt kept the camcorder
on Anna. Right now she was discussing the merits of
her new nutcracker with Kon, both of them hamming
it up a bit for the video. Lacey finally told Walter to
stop taping and join them in a final congratulatory
drink. Meg felt too nervous to swallow more than a
few mouthfuls of champagne.

Before the ceremony, she'd dreaded the arrival of
Walt and Lacey, who'd been in league with Kon from
the beginning. But now that they'd finished their toast
and were making plans to leave, Meg found she'd actually enjoyed their undemanding company and special kindness to Anna, and she didn't want them to
go—for once they did she'd be alone with Kon. Her

husband—who posed more of a personal danger to her peace of mind than ever before.

Anna hugged Lacey and thanked her for the nutcracker before she and Walt left the house in a flurry of goodbyes and Christmas wishes.

Kon shut the door behind them, then turned around, his glance sweeping over Meg's face and body. It reminded her of the many times in Russia when his gaze had said he could hardly wait to get her alone. That look had always left her shaken and trembling, and she felt no different now. Finally, to her relief, he turned to his daughter.

"Now that the wedding is over and we are an official family, I thought we'd celebrate someplace exciting."

Anna's eyes worshiped him. "Where are we going, Daddy?"

"With your mother's approval, I'd like to take us to dinner at the Molly Brown Theater to watch the Christmas show. There'll be singing and dancing and all your favorite Mark Twain characters. How does that sound?"

While Anna pleaded for her mother's acquiesence, he waited for Meg's reaction. The show catered to families with small children, and there would be other people around to act as a buffer, so Meg couldn't think of a better way to fill the next few hours. "I—I think that sounds lovely."

Kon appeared pleased by her agreement and glanced quickly at his watch. "We need to leave now if we're going to be on time."

"I'll find my coat." Anna dashed from the room and Meg hurried into the hall to catch up with her. She couldn't tolerate being alone in the same room with Kon while she was still trying to forget the taste and feel of his mouth, the passion he evoked whenever he touched her.

Over the past few days she'd managed to cope with his presence, not only because there'd been so much to do—dresses to buy and arrangements to make for the move—but because Anna and Melanie were constantly around, acting as unofficial chaperons.

And, of course, Anna had told everybody in the apartment complex about the wedding, which had prompted a number of people, including Melanie's family, the Garretts and Mrs. Rosen, to drop by with fruitcake and cookies and offer their congratulations.

Kon, who looked upon his daughter with fatherly pride whenever she played her violin for him, had taken an instant liking to Anna's teacher. He'd assured Mrs. Rosen that he'd drive Anna into St. Louis every week so she wouldn't miss her lessons. He'd also promised Anna they'd go early enough for her to spend time with Melanie. Naturally that won Melanie's overwhelming approval and devotion.

In fact, she'd spent most of Tuesday staring at Kon, following him around, plying him with questions. He answered them with infinite tolerance and good-natured humor while he dismantled the aquarium, taking care to put the fish in jars Anna had filled with water for the transfer to Hannibal.

Meg knew Anna would miss her friend, but she could tell it was going to be much more of a wrench for Melanie. The movers would be coming after Christmas to load their belongings; by New Year's, Meg and Anna would have left the complex for good.

In an effort to smooth the transition for both girls, she'd invited Melanie to come the following weekend for a sleep-over. That had naturally initiated a whole new series of conversations and plans and made the move less upsetting.

Persuaded by both Kon and Anna, Meg had resigned from her job without giving the usual two-week notice; she hoped that because business was slow during the Christmas holidays, her boss wasn't too angry with her.

Inevitably Ted had heard about Meg's impending marriage to Anna's natural father, and he called her to find out what was going on. Unfortunately Kon happened to answer the phone first, telling Ted she was too busy to talk and would call him back after they'd returned from their honeymoon.

Meg had no intention of going on a honeymoon with Kon and could just imagine Ted's reaction to that inflammatory piece of news. She decided that in a few days she'd write him a note explaining the situation. He was a nice person, and Kon had no right to intentionally offend him.

"Cold?" his deep voice murmured near her ear, startling her out of her reverie. She hadn't realized Kon had followed her and Anna into the hall. "Maybe this will warm you." His nearness made her knees go weak. Meg turned around to see Kon holding up an elegant black cashmere coat lined in black satin. "Try it on, Meggie."

As if in a trance, she put her arms into the sleeves and tied the belt around her slender waist.

"Mommy, you look *beautiful*."

"She does, doesn't she, Anochka," Kon murmured as he shrugged into a formal, dark blue topcoat. He gazed openly at Meg's ash-blond hair gleaming silvery gold against the soft black of the coat. At the question in her eyes, he smiled. "Consider it an early Christmas present."

"Thank you," she whispered, and averted her head, filled with a strange, terrible pain. Kon had decided to defect because of the many problems relating to his work in the KGB, but mostly because of Anna. And in order to have his daughter, he had to take Meg, too.

Meg didn't deceive herself. After all these years, Kon *couldn't* still be in love with her. Love had to be nurtured, and they'd been apart too many years. She had no doubt he'd told her that he hadn't been involved with another woman to spare her feelings.

He could shower her with gifts and convincingly act the lover, but it was for one reason only—she was the mother of his child. Anna was the key. He would never have come to Missouri to marry her otherwise.

Because of the way they'd once felt about each other, it was all too easy for Kon to claim that his love for her had never died, that it was too powerful and intense to die.

The unpalatable truth was that any woman who happened to be his child's mother would be the recipient of Kon's generosity. He'd waited six years before making his appearance; he'd even confessed that he'd taken the risk that she'd be married by the time he deemed it safe to present himself. That hardly sounded like a man deeply and passionately in love.

She thought back on his admissions about the other women in his life, agents working under him. Apparently none of them had gotten pregnant, and she supposed that was why he'd felt nothing lasting, why he hadn't married during all those years in the KGB.

Little did she realize when she first went to bed with him in that cottage seven years ago, her life would be irrevocably changed, that her chance to find love with a typical American man—the kind of love her mother had found with her father—would pass her by.

"Pretend to have a good time for Anna's sake, will you? It is our wedding day, after all." He spoke in a low, brusque tone meant for her ears alone as they left the dogs guarding the house and went out through the back door.

The change in his demeanor shocked her into realizing that her thoughts had been visible enough for him to read. For Anna's sake she made a mental note to avoid alienating him further.

She could tell he was still attempting to suppress his anger as he opened the front passenger door of his car. It was a Buick, the kind of car an American man named Gary Johnson might drive. Meg couldn't help but wonder what kind of car Kon would have chosen if he hadn't been forced to exist as this invented persona.

Anna's happy chatter coming from the back seat made the uncomfortable silence between the two of them even more marked. Thankfully, Meg noted that their daughter seemed oblivious to any undercurrents as they drove on streets relatively free of snow to the dinner theater situated near the riverboat landing. Kon let them out in front, then found a parking spot and joined them.

After the numbing cold outside, the building felt warm and inviting. It also looked filled to capacity, but the hostess, dressed in an 1850s' period costume, showed them to a table Kon had reserved. Located on the first level, it allowed Anna an unimpeded view of the stage show.

The next few hours flew by as they ate a delicious dinner and sat entertained by one of the actors, who did a wonderful impersonation of Mark Twain. A professionally staged musical production presented songs of the '20s through the '50s and ended with some renditions of Mississippi river music that enchanted Anna.

Meg would have loved it if she'd been here with anyone but her husband, on any day but her wedding day. Kon lounged, apparently relaxed in his seat at her side and appeared to be enjoying the performance. But when the house lights dimmed for the final act and she dared a glance at him, she saw a haunted, faraway look that hardened his features and told her he was seeing something else, thinking of another time, another place.

Perhaps for the first time since the ballet, Meg truly understood how much he must miss his country, how much he'd given up to be with his daughter.

Six years was probably an eternity to a man deprived of Russia's beautiful language and age-old culture. How lonely he must be for people like himself, his compatriots. How could he stand to live here when he was a product of a fabulous and colorful history that had produced the czars and contributed so much to world culture—to literature, music, dance and theater?

Meg had fallen in love with his country. She knew better than most how much he must be yearning for the woods and mountains of his homeland. Seven years ago he'd spent many, many hours driving Meg through rural villages and long mountain roads. Unless she specifically asked that he take her to a café or a museum, he had always headed for the countryside.

It was probably natural, since his first recollections of childhood were of Siberia, of frozen tundra in winter and wildflower meadows in summer. His home had probably been little more than a mountain hut, where life had been hard, maybe even primitive, but where there had been love....

"Tears, Meggie?" Kon mocked in quiet menace as he unexpectedly turned his head and caught her staring. "Have you suddenly realized how much of a prisoner you are now that you're legally tied to me? Are you thinking that the walls of your new home are no different from the walls of that jail cell in Moscow?"

Kon was so far off the mark she was stunned. She lowered her head to search for a clean napkin so she could wipe her eyes before Anna noticed anything was wrong.

"Gary?" A vibrant female voice spoke up just as the houselights went back on. Both Meg's and Anna's heads swiveled around as a tall, curvaceous brunette still in costume put her arms around Kon's neck and lowered her face to his. "I thought it was you. No other man that gorgeous has ever sat in this audience before."

"Sammi."

Meg was shocked that the beautiful woman's name came so easily to Kon's lips. Not only that, the two of them were so familiar with each other he actually caressed her cheek with his lips before getting to his feet.

With his arm around the actress's waist, he gazed down at Meg. She was so shattered by feelings of jealousy she could hardly move—and Kon knew it! She could tell by the way his eyes glittered. "Sammi Raynes, meet my wife, Meg, and our daughter, Anna."

Meg could tell the woman was sizing them up, trying to figure out how Kon could have a daughter this old.

"You mean you went and got married on me while I was on tour?" she cried, extending a friendly hand. "You heartbreaker!" Then she turned to Meg once more. "How do you like that? This character told me he'd be waiting for me when I got back. Your marriage happened awfully fast, didn't it?"

"Actually, K—Gary and I have known each other for a long time." Meg caught herself barely in time.

The woman's eyes flicked back to Kon. "You're a deep one, you know that?"

She was probably much closer to Kon's age than Meg was. She'd clearly had more than a casual interest in him and was putting up a heroic front. But Meg had no doubt that the actress's face had paled beneath all her stage makeup.

Had Kon been sleeping with her? And for how long?

Meg had been so focused on her own problems and fears she hadn't given any real thought to the women Kon might have met *after* defecting. Just as she'd surmised earlier, his statement that there'd been no other women since Meg had been another little fabrication, another part of his strategy. Kon wasn't the celibate type and had never pretended to be. Naturally he would indulge himself when the opportunity arose. Few women could remain immune to his virile looks and charm, as no one knew better than Meg.

Dear God, she was still in love with him. She always would be.

The woman called Sammi walked around to Anna's side. "Did you like the show, honey?"

Anna nodded. "We came here 'cause my mommy and daddy got married today."

"Today? Is that why you're wearing such a pretty dress?" When Anna nodded again, she looked at Kon for confirmation.

"That's right."

"Well, congratulations. If I'd known that before the show started, I would have asked the director to announce it. Here. Have a lollipop." She pulled one from her pocket and handed it to Anna, who asked her parents if it was all right before she accepted it.

A warm, genuine smile lit Kon's features as he smiled at the actress, and something unpleasant twisted inside Meg. She'd never seen Kon smile at *her* in quite that way, not even during those carefree days in St. Petersburg when they were alone and away from prying eyes, where he could be himself.

"Thanks, Sammi. It's always good to see you," he murmured.

"The feeling is entirely mutual."

She broke eye contact with Kon, then cast a speculative glance at Meg. "You're a lucky woman. Take good care of this marvelous man. There's no one to compare to him."

She was right, Meg acknowledged, and her pain deepened. How did Sammi know so much about him? It seemed that Kon had allowed this particular woman to see a side of him he'd never shown Meg.

Kon gave her a final hug. "One day soon we'll invite you for dinner."

"I have a new puppy you can hold," Anna offered, easily managing to talk around the lollipop still in her mouth.

"A new puppy, too? There's so much excitement at your house, I bet you can hardly get to sleep at night."

Anna giggled and Meg warmed to the woman in spite of her own distress. "I enjoyed the show very much, Ms. Raynes. We all did."

The actress smiled her thanks and moved away. Kon walked some distance with her while they talked in private. As Meg stared at their dark heads bent toward each other, a horrible envy rose up in her. Needing to expend her nervous energy, she jumped up from the table and helped Anna with her coat before slipping on her own. Ready to face the cold, they had started making their way through the crowd when Kon intercepted them.

Meg felt his eyes on her, trying to draw her gaze, but she couldn't look at him. She waited as he picked up Anna, then followed them out of the theater to the car. She made sure she didn't walk close enough for him to touch her.

"Are we going to get our Christmas tree now?" Anna asked cheerfully.

"I think we've done enough for one day, Anochka. How about tomorrow morning, after you've had a good night's sleep and a hot breakfast?"

"Okay. Who was that lady, Daddy? I saw you kiss her."

"She's a good friend."

"Do you love her, too?"

Unconsciously Meg held her breath, waiting for his answer.

"If you mean, do I love her the way I love you and your mommy, no."

"Does she love you?"

Kon crushed her in his arms. "There are all kinds of love, Anna. I met her several years ago when her little boy got lost during a family picnic. The whole town ended up looking for him. I happened to be the one who finally found him, asleep under some bushes near the Mark Twain Cave."

Meg's heart lurched in her chest.

"What's his name?" Anna persisted.

"Brad."

"How old is he?"

"Eight."

"Doesn't he have a daddy?"

"Yes, although his daddy doesn't live with them."

"How come *you* found him?"

"I was lucky."

Anna's arms tightened around Kon's neck. "I'm glad you're my daddy."

"So am I," he whispered.

So am I, Meg's heart echoed wildly.

CHAPTER EIGHT

WHEN THEY REACHED the house, Anna cuddled her puppy, then climbed the stairs to get ready for bed. Kon said that as soon as he'd taken care of the dogs and turned out the lights, he'd be up to kiss her good-night.

But the minute her curly head touched the pillow, Anna's eyes closed and she fell sound asleep, hugging the nutcracker in her arms.

Meg hung the beautiful party dress in the closet and tidied the room. When she felt it was safe, she carefully removed the nutcracker from Anna's now-slack grip and put it on the white French-provincial dresser. It matched the canopied bed and night table. The room was a fairyland of pink and white eyelet, everything a little girl's heart could desire.

After Christmas, when the movers delivered the belongings from the apartment to Kon's house, the room would be filled with all of Anna's things, including the rest of her dolls. So far, the only large item they'd brought with them was the aquarium, which Kon had immediately set up under Anna's supervision.

Meg wandered over to the tank and watched the fish, remembering the day she'd purchased the aquarium, never dreaming where it would finally end up. Since she knew Anna needed some kind of pet and animals were forbidden in the apartment building, fish had seemed a good solution.

Now her daughter had three dogs to love. And a father who returned all the love she gave him, yet could be firm with her when the occasion warranted. At first Meg had been afraid he would spoil Anna, but time was proving her wrong. He was very much in charge of their daughter, not the other way around.

Was it all a sham? Or could she dare believe that Kon would never have taken Anna away from her, even if they *hadn't* married?

"Meggie?"

There was a husky timbre in his voice that made her tremble. She lifted her head to see Kon's dark shape in the doorway.

"Yes?"

"Now that Anna's asleep, I'd like some attention."

Her fingers clung to the edge of the tank. "I—I'm coming."

Her mouth went completely dry as she followed him out to the hallway and shut the door. She noticed with alarm that he'd changed out of his clothes and was dressed in a blue-and-black-striped velour robe. She wondered, aroused yet half-ashamed, if he wore anything underneath.

It didn't matter that this same man had made love to her seven years ago. He was still an enigma to her, more now than ever. A virtual stranger. She wanted to trust him, but it was so hard....

"Before the wedding I told you the choice was yours to sleep in my bed or not."

Her nails cut into her palms. "But now that we're married, you've decided to do what you want, forget the promise you made."

"In a manner of speaking, yes. I want you in my bed, Meggie. I won't make love to you if you don't want me to, but I need you lying there next to me. Don't deny me that, *mayah labof.*"

"I'm not your darling," she gasped, so breathless she felt dizzy.

"You are. You always will be."

"No more lies, Kon. Please God, no more lies," she begged, the tears streaming from her eyes. "You said you wanted a relationship with Anna, and now you have it. Isn't that enough?"

"I wish I could say it was. But it isn't." His voice trailed off.

"And if I refuse?"

"Don't. I've waited too long."

"So now that you have me where you want me, you're flinging the mask away. Is that it?"

"There was never any mask," he said calmly, his hands in his pockets. "I begged you to marry me before you left Russia. I asked you to marry me as soon as I saw you at the ballet. You're my wife now. There's nothing to keep us apart."

"Nothing except the fact that I don't even know who you are," she half sobbed. "I don't know the first thing about you. I've never met your family. In Russia you were a highly placed, feared KGB agent, and I'll never know if our affair was part of a secret plan or not. You said your name was Konstantin Rudenko. Is that the name your parents gave you or one the KGB made up?"

Her hysteria had reached a momentum, and she couldn't stop herself. "In my country you pretend to be an ordinary American citizen named Gary Johnson. He lives in a dream house, drives a Buick and behaves like Mr. Niceguy to his unsuspecting community. How can I know the real you? Have I ever met him? Where did the child, the teenager, the young man go? Or were they ever allowed to exist? *Who are you?*" Her frantic voice broke.

His face darkened and he shook his head. "I don't know, Meggie. It's why I came for you. To find out."

The admission seemed to come from someplace deep within him, and it was the last answer she'd expected. It threw her into such confusion she didn't know how to react or what to say. It drove her to the guest room, between his bedroom and Anna's. She'd slept there the night before, tossing and turning as she anticipated her wedding day with alternating feelings of excitement and dread.

Kon stood in the doorway. "Can we start finding our answers in bed? That's where we once communicated without any problems—one man and one woman. Can we go from there?" He grasped the doorjamb as if for support. "I swear I won't touch you, Meggie, if that's the way it has to be. Only lie with me tonight." His voice throbbed with raw longing.

"After this many years' separation—" he switched to Russian so easily Meg was scarcely aware of it

"—let me have the satisfaction of at least looking at you throughout the night, smelling the flowery scent of your hair, knowing you're within arm's reach. I'm begging you, Meggie."

Speaking to her in his native tongue, in that particular tone of voice, tore down her last, pathetic defense. It brought back too many memories, memories that suffocated her with their sweetness.

Meg grabbed a nightgown from the dresser and hurried into the bathroom to change. Her heart pounded at every pulse point until she thought it might explode. This vulnerable, pleading side of Kon had left her utterly vulnerable, too.

He was still standing in the doorway when she came back into the room. He followed her with his eyes as she hung her wedding dress in the closet.

The short walk to the bed felt like a hundred miles. When she got under the covers, Kon turned off the light and moved toward her.

"Meggie?" he whispered.

"I—I don't think—"

"If I stay with you tonight," he interrupted her, "then you don't have to be afraid I'll kidnap Anna. That is what you're terrified of, isn't it?"

No, her heart cried. *I'm afraid of something much worse. I'm afraid you'll never love me the way I love you.*

The mattress dipped as he slid beneath the covers, and though their bodies didn't touch, she could feel his warmth and smell the soap that lingered on his skin. She had no idea if he'd disrobed and wished her mind couldn't see what the darkness blotted out.

"Talk to me, *mayah labof*." His low, velvety voice reached out to her like a soft night wind. "Tell me how long it took you to forget me after you left Russian soil. Had some other man fallen in love with you by the time your plane landed?"

Oh, Kon. She smothered her groan in the pillow and hugged the side of the bed.

"I watched your plane until it disappeared in the clouds, then drove back to the cottage like a demon possessed and drank enough vodka to send myself into oblivion. Or so I thought. But nothing was strong enough to wipe out your fragrance on the sheets and pillows. Dear God, Meggie—the emptiness after everything we'd shared... I didn't particularly care if I lived or died."

"Do you think I felt any different?" she blurted. Whether he was still acting a part or not, his words unlocked memories and they came flooding back with an intensity so fresh she felt as if she were reliving the nightmare. "I kept thinking that if the plane crashed, it didn't matter, which shows you the instability of my state of mind, considering that there were hundreds of other people on that flight.

"I had no one to go home to, and I'd left my heart behind. At one point during the trip home, I even found myself wishing I was dead because I couldn't bear to imagine you with another lover, particularly one of your beautiful, dark-haired Russian women. I always saw them staring at you with hungry eyes whenever we went out in public."

"Meggie!"

"They did, Kon, and you know it, so don't try to deny it. I had no idea I could be that jealous."

A heavy sigh escaped. "Think what you will, but I had eyes only for the exquisite blond creature who got off that plane in Moscow and caused complete havoc with my comrades as she passed through control. Every agent there would have given six months' pay for the privilege of being assigned to you. When they found out you were under my supervision, I acquired enemies."

If any other man had said that to her, Meg would have scoffed. Instead, she shuddered. He was probably exaggerating but . . . how would she ever know?

"Thank God your plane didn't crash," he murmured. "Tell me what exactly happened when you arrived back in the States. What you did. How you felt."

Why did he ask these questions when he already knew the answers?

Her eyes closed tightly as if to ward off the pain. By the time she'd passed through customs and the CIA had finished with her, allowing her to go free, she'd walked away feeling as if she'd been skinned alive and her heart torn from her body.

"When the plane landed in New York, I was singled out from the others and taken to a place for a grueling, two-day debriefing."

She heard his sharp intake of breath. "Because of me," he said. "Because they knew of our association."

"Yes."

"And that's when you were warned off for good."

"Yes." Frantically wiping tears from her cheeks, she said, "Up until they told me that I'd been targeted specifically by you, I had every intention of saving my money and returning to Moscow the following summer to be with you."

"Now you know why I told you never to come back," he muttered fiercely.

"It . . . it was a good thing I had so much to do after they released me, or I would have gone mad remembering my aunt's warnings. As it was, I had trouble sleeping and lost weight. I suppose what saved me was the necessity of finding an apartment and getting things out of storage. And, of course, looking for a job."

"You didn't go back to teaching."

"No. I wanted nothing to do with anything that could remind me of you. So I took the first job that offered decent pay."

"Strong Motors?"

"Yes."

"Tell me about the pregnancy. When did you first discover our baby was growing inside you?"

Taking a steadying breath, she said, "As I told you, food didn't interest me and I slept poorly. When a month passed and my condition seemed to get worse because I felt tired all the time, my friend at work urged me to see a doctor.

"I fought against taking her advice, but then I started to be sick to my stomach in the mornings and realized something was wrong. So I consulted my family doctor over the phone. When he heard the symptoms, he sent me to see an obstetrician.

"I was furious when he suggested I could be pregnant, because I knew you'd taken precautions. That was when he gave me a lecture about no contraceptive method being one hundred percent reliable. After the examination the obstetrician told me I was definitely pregnant. I didn't want to believe her."

A heavy silence hung in the air. "Did you..."

"No, Kon. I never considered an abortion, if that's what you're asking. Whatever happened between us, our baby was an innocent victim. I would never have done anything to harm it. In fact, I experienced a miraculous sense of responsibility when I learned I was pregnant. I had a reason to go on living. I followed the doctor's advice so the baby would be born strong and healthy."

"Thank you for telling me that." His whisper reached her ears. "Don't you know I'd have given my life to have been there for you?"

Could he sound that sincere and still be lying? She didn't know anymore.

"When I saw Anna's baby picture," he began, "I started working on a plan to defect, one that would expose the fewest people to danger. That had to be my first priority. Of necessity it was elaborate and had to be timed to the split second."

"How did you finally get away?" She couldn't help wanting to know the answer to that question.

"I can't tell you."

Rage welled up in her all over again, and she shot straight up in bed, pushing the hair out of her eyes. "And you still expect me to trust you?"

Kon raised himself on one elbow, as calm as a panther at rest, but capable of springing at the slightest provocation. "Don't you think I'd like to be able to tell you what I went through to join you and Anna?"

"I don't understand why you can't. I thought a husband and wife were supposed to share everything."

"So did I," came his mocking reply. "But the matter of my defection falls into another category altogether. I have to keep quiet to protect others who put their lives at risk to help me."

There was too much to absorb. "Do you think you're still under surveillance by your government?"

"Actively, no. But I'm on a list."

She had difficulty swallowing. "Does that mean you could still be in danger?"

"From which government?"

His question chilled her. "Don't tease me, Kon."

"Maybe it's better we skip the subject altogether."

"Why would you be in danger from my government?" she persisted.

"Perhaps because they don't trust me any more than you do." He reached out for her pillow and pulled it to him, burying his face for a moment.

The vulnerability and despair in that gesture made her avert her eyes. "Even after you gave them information?"

He lifted his head. "You once said it yourself. A man who could turn his back on his country is a traitor to all."

The words she'd thrown at him. They sounded cruel. If no one ever trusted him, how lonely his life must have been for the past six years. How lonely it would continue to be for the rest of his life.

He slid from the bed, still dressed in his robe. The tie had come loose, though, allowing her a glimpse of his well-defined chest with its dusting of dark hair. "I knew it was too much to hope that we could start over. But fool that I am, I had to try. Good night, Meggie."

He strode to the door, then paused. "I'll give you an early Christmas present now—by promising that I'll never ask you to sleep with me again."

"WHERE ARE WE GOING to put the tree, Daddy?"

"Wherever your mother thinks is best."

They'd gone shopping that morning. Meg had left it to Anna to entertain Kon while they'd gone into store after store, looking for more tree decorations. The lights and ornaments from the small Scotch pine they'd dismantled at the apartment would only cover part of the eight-foot tree they'd purchased.

But now that they were home, Meg couldn't go on ignoring Kon. Anna listened to every word and nuance of meaning, observed everything that passed between her parents. So Meg stated that the best spot might be in front of the living-room window. Everyone driving by would see their tree. All they had to do was move the table and lamp to a different place.

The suggestion met with wholehearted approval, and Kon, dressed in jeans and sweater, set up the perfectly shaped blue spruce in a matter of minutes. As soon as Meg untangled a set of lights, Anna, with Thor at her heels, handed them to her father and he strung them on the tree. The three of them worked in complete harmony. Anyone peeking in the window would see the ideal family happily at work.

No one could know of the brooding blackness in Kon or suspect that after he'd left her room last night, Meg had lain awake in agony, part of her wanting, aching, to go to him and crawl into his arms.

But something intangible had occurred during their conversation. The man who had devastated her by promising he'd never ask her to sleep with him again was not the same man who earlier that night had begged her to lie next to him, just to know she was there.

Lacking the confidence to face him in case he rejected her attempt at reconciliation, she remained in her bed, alone. She spent the rest of the night trying to sort out her own confused thoughts and feelings.

Every time she attempted to put herself in his place, she felt physically ill. She could imagine his sense of isolation, the inevitable gloom and depression that must have weighed him down after leaving Russia to settle in a country as foreign and unfamiliar as the United States.

The CIA had given her some things to read, articles about defectors years before; she remembered that one theme had dominated the rest. They lived with the consequences of displacement for the rest of their lives.

Perhaps that explained why Kon had become the exemplary father, throwing himself into the role so completely. Perhaps that way he could forget for a short period what he'd left behind. It would also explain why he'd wanted Meg in his bed last night, to blot out for a brief time the pain of his actions.

In all honesty, she had to admit she couldn't blame him for those very human needs and drives. If their positions were reversed and she could never return to the United States, it would be a horrifying experience, one she'd have to sublimate somehow, just as he was doing.

"Mommy, you forgot to open the last box."

Startled out of her tortured thoughts, Meg tore off the cellophane and handed the lights to Anna. In an unguarded moment, her glance darted to Kon, who seemed to stare right through her, as if his thoughts were far removed from the scene in front of him. Cold fear spread through her body—there was such unhappiness in his look, and a kind of bleak resignation. Meg couldn't stand it. She excused herself to start dinner.

During the next few days a feeling of domestic tranquillity existed, on the surface, at least. But Kon had withdrawn emotionally from Meg, and she was paying a bitter price. Upset and confused by this remote stranger who'd never treated her with such indifference before, she needed to do something, anything, to relieve the tension between them.

It was on one of her trips with Anna back to the apartment to finish cleaning that Meg scanned a batch of Christmas cards sent to her and came across one from Tatiana Smirnov, her old Russian teacher. The woman's newsy letter triggered an idea for a special Christmas present for Kon, one she hoped would let him know she understood the loneliness of his self-imposed exile and wanted to make up for it in some small way.

When Ken came to pick them up, Meg told him that as long as they were in St. Louis, she and Anna had a few more presents to buy. He dropped them off at a local mall, indicating that he needed to take care of some business and would be back for them in a couple of hours.

The minute he was out of sight, Meg explained her secret to Anna. Then she hailed a taxi and gave the driver an address that took them across town to an art gallery Tatiana had mentioned in her letter. A shipment of arts and crafts from Russia was up for sale. Meg and Anna spent a good hour studying the paintings, icons, dolls, hats, scarves, eggs—all kinds of memorabilia from bygone eras.

As many times as Meg went over everything, her eye kept going back to one particular oil painting. It depicted a mountain scene with a meadow of wildflowers in the foreground. Her gaze followed the dirt road that ran past an old barn, then disappeared. The painting's title, printed in Russian, convinced her. *Urals in springtime.*

Anna was taken with several of the icons but preferred the one of the Madonna and child. The combination of colors—gold and royal blue against the black of the shiny wood—drew the eye, and Meg told the saleswoman to wrap it up along with the painting.

Out of Anna's hearing she also whispered to the clerk to include the nesting doll sitting on the display table. The pink-and-black stylized figure of a Russian peasant woman hid seven versions of the same woman, each one smaller than the one before. They all fit together, and Anna would be delighted when she discovered the surprise.

The clerk put it in a sack, and when Anna wasn't looking, Meg stuffed it into her tote bag. The purchases cost more than a thousand dollars and took most of Meg's meager savings. But the situation between her and Kon had grown so precarious she would have done anything to extend the olive branch.

They took another taxi back to the mall, where they stopped to get their gifts boxed and wrapped in beautiful Christmas paper at a gift-wrapping booth. Then they window-shopped until Kon came for them.

Though Anna was bursting to tell her father what they'd done and wanted to give him his presents right then and there, she managed to contain herself. But her eyes sparkled like blue topaz, and Kon's gaze slid to Meg's several times in silent query. The amused glimmer in his eyes made her heart turn over, their enmity temporarily forgotten in the face of their daughter's excitement.

On Christmas Eve another winter storm blanketed the area with snow, delighting Anna. Along with the dogs, she followed her father outside, watching while he shoveled the driveway and then built her a snowman. As Meg gazed out at them from the dining room window where she was setting the table for their Christmas dinner, she saw that a couple of children close to Anna's age had come by to help.

There were joyous shouts mingled with the dogs' barking, and Kon seemed to be having as much fun as the children who hovered around him.

Seeing him like this, Meg had to ask herself again—what if he was exactly what he seemed? A man who'd willingly made certain choices. A loving father. A new American citizen who embraced the land he'd chosen. A man who still loved a woman, although seven years had passed. What if there were no ulterior motives and everything he'd been telling her all this time was the absolute truth? Tears stung her eyes....

Meg couldn't sleep that night. Long after she'd slipped downstairs at midnight to put her presents under the tree, she lay wide awake in the large bed, staring into the darkness as the tears ran down her face.

Early Christmas morning Anna ran into Meg's room with both dogs at her heels, bubbling with excitement. Daddy was already up fixing breakfast, she said. According to him, Santa had come, and as soon as they'd eaten, they could go into the living room and see what he'd brought.

A feeling not unlike morning sickness assailed Meg as she got out of bed and staggered to the bathroom. After spending most of the night crying until she wondered how there could be any more tears, she was sure that facing Kon, let alone Christmas day, was almost beyond her. But she had to, for Anna's sake.

The shower revived her a little. She brushed her hair and secured it with combs at both sides, then added blusher to her pale cheeks, followed by an application of lipstick. She pulled on a cherry-red sweater dress she'd had for a couple of years. Her low black patent pumps would be comfortable to walk around in and still look dressy.

"Just keep coming toward me," Kon murmured as she started down the stairs, the camcorder in his hands. "Merry Christmas, Meggie."

"Merry Christmas," she said when she could find the words. The sight of his dark, handsome features, his snug-fitting forest-green sweater and charcoal pants, his lithe movements left her breathless.

Anna stood next to her father in a new dress of red-and-blue plaid, a glowing look of anticipation on her face. "You have to kiss Daddy, Mommy, 'cause Daddy says it's a tradition."

"Only if she wants to, Anochka."

Meg needed no urging to close the distance between them and rise on tiptoe to brush her mouth against his. Kon would never be able to guess at the depth of her hunger for him, the kind of iron control it took not to devour him in front of their daughter. It was no use pretending that she didn't remember every second of those months when he'd been her lover.

His passion had electrified her, bringing them both a fullness of joy she hadn't known was possible.

Heaven help her. She wanted to know that joy again.

CHAPTER NINE

"CAN WE GO IN NOW, Daddy? I've eaten my eggs and drunk all my milk."

"What do you say, Meggie? Are we ready?"

She lifted her eyes to surprise a bleak look in his. It was only there for a moment, but she couldn't have been mistaken and it only added to her torment.

With a nod she put her coffee cup back on the saucer. "Why don't I get the two of you on tape first?"

Not waiting for a reply, she jumped up from the table and grabbed the camcorder from the counter, preceding them into the living room.

The next hour flew by. The dogs crouched close to Anna, who squealed in ecstasy over the new dollhouse and tea set Kon had set up for her. Meg had hidden the nesting doll in Anna's stocking, along with a candy cane and an inexpensive Little Mermaid watch.

Anna shook everything out, then examined the strange-looking toy first. "What is it, Mommy? An old lady?"

Meg laughed because her daughter didn't know what to make of it. Kon's delighted chuckle joined hers, and he threw Meg a quizzical glance, as if to ask her where she'd found the Russian treasure. The sound of lazy amusement in his voice as he talked to his daughter reminded her sharply of other times and places. A time, seven years ago, when she'd been madly in love with him and free to express that love. A night at her hotel in St. Petersburg, when he'd been lounging on the floor at her feet, just like this. Only now it was Anna's face he caressed, her bouncing curls he tousled.

"Watch this, Anochka."

In a deft movement that fascinated Meg, as well, Kon pulled the two halves of the doll apart. Anna saw a smaller version of the same doll inside and cried out in wonder.

"Open it like I did," Kon urged.

Within a few minutes fourteen halves lay spread out on the carpet, and Anna sat there with a frown of concentration on her face, trying to put everything back together again.

Meg decided now was the time to give Kon her present. "I hope you'll like this," she said in a nervous voice, wondering too late if it was the wrong thing to give him. Maybe he wouldn't want a reminder of everything he'd left behind.

He took the package from her hands and sat up to remove the paper. Anna was too aborbed with the dolls to notice how quiet the room had become, but Meg felt uncomfortably aware of the unnatural stillness. She held her breath while Kon studied the canvas. What was he thinking?

"I-it's a scene in the Urals. You must be missing Russia, and since you said you liked to hike there, I thought—"

"Meggie..." Where he gripped the edge of the canvas, his knuckles stood out white.

"I have a present for you, too, Daddy."

Anna dropped the doll parts she was having problems fitting together and scurried around the far side of the tree to fetch the package.

When she handed it to him, he put it to his ear and shook it, making Anna giggle. "I wonder what my little Anochka has given me."

Anna couldn't wait any longer. "It's an . . . an icon, isn't it, Mommy?"

Kon's grin slowly faded to be replaced by a sober expression as he carefully lifted the wooden plaque from the tissue and reverently traced the halos of gold with his index finger, his head bent in solemn concentration.

Anna squeezed past the dogs and knelt down next to her father. "That's the baby Jesus with his mommy," she pointed out. "I liked this one the best. Mommy said it came from Russia. Do you think it's pretty, Daddy?"

He drew Anna roughly into his arms and buried his face in her dark curls. "I love it," came the husky reply. "I love it almost as much as I love you."

Several Russian endearments whispered in hushed tones brought tears to Meg's eyes, and she covered her emotions by busying herself opening a box of candy from her boss, and another from Ted.

"Where's Mommy's present?" Anna finally asked.

"Your father already gave it to me," she said before he could reply. "Remember the beautiful black coat I wore to the theater the other night?"

Anna nodded.

In a quick movement Kon got to his feet. "Actually, I do have another gift for your mother, but it didn't arrive in time for Christmas."

"No, please." She gathered a basket of fruit—from Mrs. Rosen—in the crook of her arm and headed for the kitchen to check on the turkey, avoiding the intensity of his gaze. "I don't want anything else. You've done too much for us already."

Relieved that he didn't follow her, she was able to get preparations under way for Christmas dinner. Anna brought her dollhouse into the kitchen and, chattering away, put a different nesting doll in each room. She gave the dolls exacting instructions on how to behave. If they didn't, she said, the nutcracker, who stood guard on one of the kitchen chairs, would have to punish them.

Eventually her new friends from across the street traipsed through the house to see her presents and look at the puppies still confined to the porch. They were all fascinated by the nesting doll, and at one point Kon had to intervene so everyone could take turns assembling the various parts.

Finally the children grew tired of even that game, and at Kon's suggestion they decided to play outside in the snow, leaving Meg in peace.

Once everything was cooking, she went to the living room to clean up the mess, but Kon had gotten there before her and the room looked immaculate. He'd put the painting and the icon on the mantel and had started a fire in the grate. She felt compelled to find him and thank him.

When he wasn't in his study she called to him from the foot of the stairs, but there was no answer. Nor was there any sign of Prince, or Thor and Gandy, whose other two pups had been given to a family across the street. Whirling around, she ran out the back of the house, but no one responded when she called and both cars were still in the garage.

Maybe everyone was in the front yard. She ran down the driveway, almost losing her balance in her heels while she shouted for Anna. Whichever direction she looked, there was no one in sight. Nothing but snow. Freezing air lodged in her lungs as she beheld the lone snowman with one of Kon's ties around its neck.

Silent testimony to a kidnapping?

A growing dread gnawed at her insides, and she raced across the street without thought of boots or coat, praying she was wrong, praying Anna was at the neighbor's house. But when the children answered the door, they said Anna had gone off with her daddy and the dogs.

By the time Meg reached the house to get her car keys, she was hysterical with fear. She backed slowly out of the driveway and drove up and down the icy streets, past the local parks, asking people if they'd seen a man and a little girl walking a pair of German shepherds and a puppy. No one had.

Realizing there wasn't another second to lose, she sped home as fast as she could and dashed into the house, her only thought to contact the police and prevent Kon from leaving the country with their daughter. He could be anywhere by now, following another elaborate plan of escape.

With tears gushing down her cheeks, she clutched the receiver and punched in 911. When she explained that her daughter was missing, the dispatcher asked for her address and said a couple of officers would be arriving shortly.

To Meg, the next few minutes felt like centuries. Though she knew it was hopeless, something made her go out to the street and call Anna's name at the top of her lungs.

Soon the two neighbor children and their parents joined her and volunteered to start a door-to-door search. Meg thanked them, but didn't tell them she suspected Kon was behind her daughter's disappearance. That was a matter for the police. A cruiser finally drove up in front and two officers followed her into the hallway to get a statement.

"Just calm down, ma'am, and tell us why you think your family is missing. How long have they been gone?"

"I don't know. An hour or so. I was busy in the kitchen before I realized I couldn't hear voices. Even the dogs are missing."

"Maybe they went for a walk."

"Naturally I thought of that, but I've been driving around the neighborhood and there's no sign of them. No one has seen them. Our other car is still in the garage."

"Maybe they stopped at a neighbor's home. It is Christmas Day, you know."

She took a shuddering breath. "You don't understand. My husband—"

"—is right here." A chilling male voice that could only be Kon's cut her off abruptly.

"We've been at Fred's house showing him the new puppy, Mommy. He has a bottle with a ship in it and a marmalade cat who's so fat she just sleeps." Anna rushed through the hall to explain and gave her mother a huge hug while the dogs circled them, whining a little. Meg couldn't speak. She simply clutched her daughter closer.

One of the officers nodded to Kon. "Your wife here got a little nervous because you and your daughter had been gone a while."

She'd seen pain in Kon's eyes before, but nothing could compare to the look of raw anguish she saw there now. The inner light faded completely, as if something in him had just died.

Another kind of fear tore at her heart. *What had she done?*

He glanced at the officer. "You know how it is when you've only been married five days. We don't like to be out of each other's sight."

Once again, Kon's superb playacting was in evidence and he handled the awkward situation like a master. But Meg knew nothing would ever be the same between them again.

He slid his arm around her shoulders and pulled her close, pressing a fervent kiss to her temple. "Fred Dykstra was on his front porch and he called to us. His house is two doors down. He's a retired widower from the railroad and he lives alone. When he saw Anna, he invited her in to give her a chocolate Santa."

"I'm sorry," Meg whispered in agony. "I—I didn't realize..."

He rubbed her arm. "When he helped me move in, he had to put up with my talking about you and Anna all the time, and he wants to meet you. So I was coming back to the house to ask if we could invite him for dinner. That's when Anna and I saw the police car and bumped into Mrs. Dunlop, who said you were looking for us. I'm sorry if you were worried."

This time he lowered his mouth to hers in a gesture the officers would interpret as a lover's salute. In reality Kon pressed a hard, soulless kiss against her lips, a kiss that made a mockery of the passion they'd once shared. "I make you a solemn vow that I'll never be that thoughtless again, Mrs. Johnson."

Meg knew he was saying one thing while he meant another. She couldn't seem to stop shaking. No amount of sorrow or remorse for her actions would put them back on the same footing they'd achieved that morning. Before she'd called the police.

"We'll be going, then." The officer smiled. "Merry Christmas."

"Sorry to have troubled you. Merry Christmas." Kon's fingers bit into her upper arm before he released her to see them to the door.

"Anna, run out to the porch and take off your boots, honey. You're getting water on the floor."

"Okay, Mommy. Here, Thor. Here, Gandy."

Meg was halfway up the stairs when she heard Kon's footsteps and realized there was no hope of escape. He followed her into the bedroom and shut the door too quietly. He didn't say anything, merely watched her through narrowed eyes.

"I-I'm sorry," she began haltingly. "I know that sounds inadequate but—"

"Just tell me one thing," he demanded coldly. "Did you give away my cover?"

She shook her head in denial, staring at the floor. "No."

"The truth, Meggie. If you even hinted that I might have abducted her, we'll have to move and I'll be forced to take on a new identity. As it is, I'll have to get hold of...certain people to report the incident. The decision might well be out of my hands already."

His words made her more frantic than ever. "No, Kon. When I phoned 911, I only said Anna was missing. I told the Dunlops the same thing."

"But you were on the verge of telling them all about me when I walked in the hall. Don't deny it."

She struggled for the words that might placate him. There were none. "I won't," she finally murmured.

"You've missed your calling, Meggie."

She lifted tearful eyes to him and shrank from his cold, hard face.

"No Mata Hari of my acquaintance could have pulled off a more convincing act than you did this morning when you tried to give me back a little piece of my Russian soul. To include our innocent little Anna in the subterfuge was pure genius. My compliments, *beloved*." He said the endearment with a particularly cruel twist that brought a moan to her lips. "You actually had me convinced there was hope."

Unspeakable emotion—anger and something else she couldn't define—tautened every muscle and sinew of his body before he strode swiftly from the room.

When she thought about what she'd done and the possible consequences to Kon's safety after the years it had taken him to establish his new identity, Meg collapsed on the bed.

"Mommy?"

Meg could hear Anna's footsteps on the stairs. She jumped up from the bed and hurried into the bathroom to wash her face so her daughter wouldn't suspect anything.

"Can Fred come to our house for dinner? He's nice."

As far as Meg was concerned, a guest would provide the diversion she needed to get through the rest of the day. Kon had extended the initial invitation and would have to be on his best behavior.

"Of course he can, honey. Why don't you take the dogs and go back to his house and bring him over? He can spend the day with us and sit by the fire. You can show him your toys."

"Can I go right now?"

"Yes. Don't forget your hat and boots."

"I won't."

Meg followed her down the stairs and busied herself in the kitchen until she heard Anna and the dogs leaving.

Realizing Kon needed to be told about Fred, she hurried to his study. But the glacial look he shot her when she appeared in the doorway froze her into stillness.

"Where's Anna?"

Meg tried to swallow, but her throat felt swollen. "I sent her over to Mr. Dykstra's to bring him back for dinner. That's what I was coming in here to tell you."

He leaned back in his chair and watched her through shuttered eyes. "I'm glad she's out of the house for a few minutes. What I have to say won't take long, but I don't want her privy to it."

"D-did you pho—"

"I don't intend to answer any of your questions," he cut in brutally. "All you have to do is listen."

"I'm your wife!" she cried, aghast. "You have no right to speak to me like that, no matter what's happened."

"I forgot." He smiled with cold disdain. "Yes, you're my wife—who five days ago in this very house swore before God to love and honor me, be my comfort, my haven, my refuge—"

"Stop it!" she shouted. "I can't take any more."

He sucked in a breath and got to his feet. "You won't have to. I'm leaving."

"What?"

"Your name is on my bank account. You can draw out funds any time you need to. There's enough to keep you indefinitely. The house is in your name, as well."

"What do you mean?" she asked, panicking. "What are you talking about? Where are you going?"

His mouth thinned. "If I told you, you wouldn't believe me, so there's no point."

"H-how long will you be gone?"

"If it were up to you, I'd never come back, so it really doesn't matter."

She let out a groan. "Don't say that. It *does* matter. You can't do this to Anna."

"She'll recover. I was torn from my family when I was young, and I turned out all right. The Party has given me several commendations. Besides, she has *you.*"

"Kon...don't do this." She suddenly felt afraid for him. "Have I put you in danger?" When he didn't reply, she asked, "Do you hate me so much for what I did that you can't bear the sight of me any longer? Is that what this is all about?"

"I'll leave tonight after Anna has gone to sleep." He went on talking as if she hadn't spoken. "As far as she has to know, I've gone to New York on business."

"What business?" Her voice shook.

"Have you finally decided to show a little interest in my writing career?" The contempt in his question devastated her. "Did you think that was made up? That I defected to a life of luxury, living off the proceeds of the information I brought your government?"

Before they were married, she'd assumed exactly that. But too late she knew it wasn't the truth.

In a dull voice she asked, "What is it exactly that you write? Walt Bowman, or whoever he is, said something about the KGB and..." Her voice faded.

One dark brow lifted. "When I'm gone, you can search through my study to your heart's content and figure it out for yourself. At least when we part this time, Anna will have some videos to help her remember her father. It's more than I was given when I was taken away."

Meg could feel him slipping beyond her reach and didn't have the faintest idea how to hold on to him. In desperation she said, "I thought you loved Anna. I thought you defected because of her, for her."

"Does it really matter what either of us thought when it's abundantly clear I got here six years too late?" His eyes bored holes into her.

"Now, if I'm not mistaken, I can hear Thor and Gandy, which means Anna and Fred are almost at our front door. Shall we greet our guest together, *mayah labof?*"

"MRS. JOHNSON? Senator Strickland here."

Thank God. Meg's hand tightened on the receiver and she sat up in bed, praying Anna had finally gone to sleep and hadn't heard the phone ring. Today—the day after Christmas—had been a waking nightmare, one she never wanted to live through again.

"Thank you for returning my call. Thank you," she murmured. "I'd almost given up hope that you'd even get your messages before you went back to your office next week."

"I have a secretary who monitors my calls in case of an emergency. She phoned me at home when she heard your name."

"Please forgive me for bothering you this late, but I'm desperate." Her voice wobbled despite herself. "I need your help."

"This sounds serious. By a strange coincidence, my wife and I were just talking about you newlyweds on our way home from a concert tonight. We were trying to decide on a date for that dinner I promised you.''

Meg groaned with renewed pain. ''Senator—my husband left me last night.''

There was a prolonged silence on the other end of the phone. ''A domestic quarrel?''

''No. It was something that goes much deeper. I don't even know where to begin. I've been out of my mind with grief, and my daughter is inconsolable. I've got to find him and tell him I love him.'' She broke down sobbing and it took her a minute to get control of her emotions and her voice. ''He has to come back to us. *He has to.*''

''Tell me what happened.''

More hot tears streamed down her face. ''I drove him away with my paranoia. I accused him of planning to kidnap Anna and take her back to Russia.'' In a few words she explained why she'd called the police. ''All this time I've refused to believe what was before my very eyes. I have to go to him and beg his forgiveness.''

''Did he leave in his own car?''

''Yes.''

''I'll get on it as soon as we hang up, and when I have any information, I'll contact you, but I doubt it will be before morning.''

''Thank you. I'm in your debt,'' she said fervently.

''If I can effect a reunion between the two of you, then I'll hold you to that at campaign time. Meanwhile, don't give up.''

''I'll never do that,'' she vowed. ''I fell in love with him when I was seventeen. I'll always love him.''

"That's the most painful kind of love, first love," he said kindly. "Your husband told me he was similarly affected when he met you for the first time."

Meg blinked. "Kon told you that?"

"Mmm. Tell me, are you familiar with the story in the Bible about Jacob who loved Rachel?"

Her heart began hammering. "Yes."

"When your husband and I talked, I told him his plight struck me as being very much like Jacob's. He loved Rachel on sight and worked seven years for her. And even though he was tricked into marrying Leah because of the laws of the land, he loved Rachel so much he worked another seven years for her. Few women will ever know that kind of devotion from a man."

After a slight pause he went on, "Despite the laws of his former country, your husband has worked close to seven years for you, putting himself in grave danger. It hardly stands to reason that you've lost him now, no matter how dark things look at the moment."

"Thank you," she whispered tearfully. "I needed to hear that. Good night, Senator."

The minute she hung up the phone, she got out of bed and crept down the stairs to Kon's study in search of a Bible. If memory served her correctly, she'd seen one with his collection of books when she'd gone in there earlier to go through his papers. Naturally his work was stored on disk, but she found enough correspondence in the file cabinets to realize he wrote not only about the KGB but about the beauty, the culture, of Russia.

When she found the Bible, she sat down at his desk and opened it to Genesis 29. Verse 20 had been underlined in black ink and she skipped to it immediately.

And Jacob served seven years for Rachel; and they seemed unto him but a few days, for the love he had to her.

Suddenly the letters blurred together. She laid her head down on the table and wept.

CHAPTER TEN

"I DON'T WANT to go to my new school, Mommy. Prince will cry, and what if Daddy comes home and can't find me?"

It was going on three weeks since the Christmas holidays. Every single one of those days, Meg had been listening to Anna's tearful arguments repeated over and over again like a litany.

If Meg hadn't gone to Anna's new school with her every day and stayed in the building to work as a volunteer aide—so Anna could check throughout the day to make sure her mommy was still there—Anna would never have gone at all.

In truth, Meg wouldn't have let Anna go if she hadn't been able to spend the better part of the day with her at school. The yawning emptiness of the home Kon had created for them was unbearable without him. His absence affected everything and everyone, especially the dogs. They kept returning to Kon's study and whining, the sound eerily human, when they couldn't find him.

From the first night after his disappearance, Anna had crept into Meg's bed with her nutcracker and she'd been sleeping there ever since. Meg knew it would create more problems down the road, but she drew comfort from Anna's warm little body next to hers and didn't try to make her sleep on her own. It wouldn't have worked, anyway; Anna couldn't tolerate even a brief separation from her right now. Kon had been too wonderful a husband and father in the short week they'd lived together as a family. It was no wonder that Meg and Anna had gone into mourning and refused to be consoled.

Meg had no doubts that Senator Strickland had done everything in his power to discover Kon's whereabouts. Lacey Bowman had phoned Meg the morning after the senator's call. The only information the CIA would give Meg was that Kon was no longer in the country.

Because of Anna, Meg couldn't give in to the pain of that excruciating revelation. She had to go on pretending he was away on an extended business trip with his publisher and would come home just as soon as he could.

Every time the phone rang, Anna ran to get it and cried, "Daddy?" This happened so many times Meg thought her heart would break. She had to admonish her daughter to say hello first or she wouldn't be allowed to answer the phone at all.

So far, there'd been two disastrous sleep-overs with Melanie, who was so taken with Prince she never wanted to go home. But Anna was no longer the vivacious friend she used to be and refused to share her puppy. This, in turn, created fighting and unpleasantness. After Melanie left, Anna confided to Meg that she didn't want Melanie to come to her house anymore. Jason and Abby across the street were her friends now. Meg decided to let it go for the moment. She'd arrange something with Melanie in a few months' time.

Violin lessons were out, after Anna cried all day and night over having to leave the house to drive to St. Louis. It was too far away and her daddy might come home.

By the end of January, there was still no sign of him, and Meg had to face the dreadful truth that he might never come home. The more she thought about it, the more she believed he hadn't gone back to Russia at all but was looking for another place to live.

Kon spoke several European languages and could easily have relocated in Germany or Austria or even France. The American government would have co-operated with the country he'd chosen, giving him the proper papers and credentials to start over again.

And it was Meg's fault. She felt as though her heart had died.

Since Anna's inability to deal with her loss seemed to be growing worse, Meg's family doctor advised her to consult a good child psychologist and referred her to a colleague who practiced in Hannibal. Their first appointment would be the next Saturday at eleven. Meg recognized that she was in need of help herself and decided they could both benefit. She prayed counseling would help them; she could think of no other alternatives.

On Friday night after dinner, Meg broached the subject with Anna, who didn't like the fact that her mother had a doctor's appointment. Yet she had no choice but to go along, since she wouldn't let Meg out of her sight. Meg was in the process of explaining why they had to see this doctor when the doorbell rang.

"Daddy!" Anna shrieked, and toppled her chair in her haste to get to the front door. The dogs got there even faster, barking more loudly than usual.

Meg's adrenaline kicked in the way it always did—because there was a part of her that never gave up hope, either. But there was no point in telling Anna that if her father *had* come home, he would enter through the back porch from the garage. He wouldn't ring the front doorbell.

In all probability, it was Jason or Abby. Meg expected them to come running through the kitchen to play with Prince, who needed Kon's firm hand to learn obedience. Or it might be Fred, who'd become a welcome visitor and friend and had more influence with Anna than anyone else these days.

Meg was halfway to the front hall when she heard a woman's voice speaking a torrent of Russian. *"mayah malyenkyah muishka,"* she repeated. "My darling little mouse," she said over and over again.

What on earth?

Meg emerged from the dining room in time to see an elderly, heavyset woman dressed in black envelop Anna in her arms. The stranger's long gray hair was fastened in a bun, and she wore amber around her neck and wrist. Tears streamed down her ruddy cheeks, and she held on to Anna as if she'd never let her go.

"Anochka." A deep, commanding, familiar voice sounded from the front porch. "This is your babushka, but you can call her Grandma Anyah."

"Her name is just like mine!"

"That's right, Anochka. It must be fate. She's come all the way from Siberia to live with us."

Kon.

As Meg mouthed his name, he stepped into the hallway. The sight of his tall, lean body and striking face was so wonderful she could only stare and go on staring. His dazzling blue eyes were trained on her now, but there was a humble look in them she'd never seen before.

"Meggie, may I present my *matz,*" he said in a tremulous voice.

His mother.

"She's my belated Christmas present to you. She doesn't speak any English, but we'll help her learn it, won't we?"

Meg didn't answer the unspoken plea in his unshed tears, because love had lent her feet wings. She threw herself into Kon's arms so hard it might have knocked the wind out of a less solid man. Like a powerful waterfall, her avowals of love, her pleas for forgiveness, cascaded down on him, submerging him so completely he could be in no doubt that she belonged to him heart and soul.

Meg could tell the exact moment Kon knew that trust had come to stay. He groaned his satisfaction and, in full view of his mother and Anna, found Meg's questing mouth and kissed her with all the fiery passion of those halcyon days in Russia long ago. Once again they were free to give in to their hunger, their longings. Meg forgot everything but the feel of his arms and mouth, the warmth of his hard body melding to hers.

"Are you and Daddy making a baby?"

Anna!

Kon had the presence of mind to break off their kiss faster than Meg did, but he refused to let her go. He rocked her in his arms as he rested his chin on her shoulder and spoke to his daughter.

"Tomorrow, your mommy and I are going to sit down with you and explain about babies. Right now I want her to meet *my* mommy."

In a lightning move he turned Meg around, sliding his hands down her arms before wrapping his own around her waist from behind and squeezing her so every part of their bodies touched.

"Mama, this is Meggie. My wife." His voice broke as he introduced them in Russian.

Kon's mother was still holding Anna as she lifted her head from her granddaughter's curls.

Meg gasped softly when the brilliant blue eyes so like Kon's wandered over her face and hair in a friendly yet searching perusal.

It wasn't just the eyes. Her bone structure was similar to Kon's, and Meg could see flecks of dark among her gray eyebrows that testified where he'd received his black-brown hair.

Slowly the older woman put Anna down and cupped Meg's face with her hands.

"Mayah Doch," she said like a benediction.

My daughter.

Meg nodded before returning the greeting. *"Mayah Matz."*

Then they embraced. Meg formally kissed both cheeks, feeling an overwhelming tide of love and happiness. She held her mother-in-law in her arms for a long, long time. This wonderful woman who'd given birth to Kon, who'd thought he was dead all these years. This woman Meg had always wanted to meet...

Who knew the hardships, the deprivation, she'd lived through? How Meg would have loved to witness the reunion of mother and son!

There were too many questions she wanted answered, but now wasn't the time, not when everyone's emotions were spilling over. The dogs were no less thrilled as they rubbed their heads against Kon's legs in joyous homecoming.

"I'm glad you're home, Daddy. I've been waiting and *waiting* for you."

"So have I, Anochka, so have I."

By now Anna was in her father's arms, the healing after separation already begun. He whispered the special endearments he reserved for his daughter.

Anna was exactly where Meg longed to be. He was their safety, their rock, the light of their lives. Their love.

Slowly, over one gray and one dark head, Meg felt the burning heat of Kon's desire reach out to her, and she read the unspoken message in those smoldering eyes. Like her, he was barely holding on to his control until they could be alone.

But there were his mother and Anna to consider. By tacit agreement they decided to see to their comforts first. Meg's time with her husband would have to come later. Like Jacob and Rachel, they'd waited this long and could wait a little longer. But only just a little.

She answered his unasked question in a husky voice. "We'll put your mother in the room I was using before you left. It's all made up and ready for her. She'll enjoy the privacy of her own bathroom, and Anna will love having her grandmother next door."

He lowered Anna to the floor, his chest heaving with the strength of emotions he was having difficulty holding in check. "Where are your things?"

She could hardly breathe. "Where do you think?"

"They're in your room." Anna giggled. "You're silly, Daddy."

He tousled her dark curls and muttered in Russian, "Our little pitcher has awfully big ears."

Meg replied in kind with a straight face. "She takes after her father."

"And my Dimitri takes after *his* father," Anyah added. Kon grinned at Meg's astonishment.

The moment also gave Meg a glimpse of the older woman's sense of humor. It warmed her heart as nothing else could have done, and she hugged her mother-in-law once more before fastening loving eyes on her husband. "Is that your real name? Dimitri?"

"Da," his mother answered for him. "Dimitri Leudonovitch."

"How do you like it, *mayah labof?*"

"Enough to give it to our son when he's born."

She watched him swallow several times, and he looked at her with fierce longing.

Meg smiled into his eyes. "You've been gone forever, so you'd better plan to make up for lost time."

Anyah patted Meg's arm. "I can see you are good for my Dimitri. He needs to be loved by a woman like you, a woman to match his passion."

Her blunt, outspoken manner brought a blush to Meg's cheeks. To cover her embarrassment she said, "Did you know he was your son when you first saw him?"

"Da." She nodded, eyeing him with motherly pride. "No child in Shuryshkary had such a face and blue eyes like my little Deema's. And you see the way his hair grows into that widow's peak, and the shape of his ears, like a seashell?"

Her weatherworn hand reached out to touch his left eyebrow, as if she, too, couldn't get enough of him. "See the little scar covered by the hair? He got that scar and the one on his left shoulder when he fell out of a tree. I think he was four. He always loved the trees and begged his papa to take him up into the mountains we could see from our house."

Kon still loved the trees and the mountains, Meg thought, reacting with a shaky breath. She'd noted all those physical characteristics of Kon's when they'd made love. Particularly the scar on his shoulder, the one he couldn't remember getting, the one she'd kissed again and again because she loved everything about his magnificent body.

Right then Kon's eyes captured hers—hot, glowing, blue coals that let her know he was remembering the same thing she was.

Meg cleared her throat. Switching to English, she asked, "Where is Shuryshkary?"

"In northern Siberia at the foot of the Urals."

"That explains so much," she whispered.

Kon nodded his dark head and they communed in silence. But not for long, because Anna inserted herself between her parents and grandmother. "What's that sure-scary word mean?"

Kon chuckled. "It's the town where I was born, Anochka."

Unable to contain her curiosity any longer, Meg cried, "How did you ever find your mother?"

"When the idea first came to defect, I managed—with the help of another agent who owed me some favors—to get into my file. Once I read the details, I found out my mother was still alive, and I negotiated her escape with the help of your government. But like the situation with you and Anna, I had to wait all this time before I felt it was safe to bring her here. Unfortunately there were problems that prevented her from arriving on Christmas Day as we'd originally planned."

"Oh, Kon . . ." Her voice shook. Now that she had answers, his behavior on Christmas Day and his subsequent disappearance made complete sense. She lifted pleading eyes to him. "Can you ever forgi—"

"All that's over, Meggie," he broke in. "Today is the beginning of the rest of our lives."

"Yes," she whispered, and linking her arm through her mother-in-law's, she said in Russian, "Are you tired? Would you like to go upstairs, or would you like to freshen up for dinner first, then take a tour of your son's house?"

The older woman looked thoughtful. "We flew all the way from San Francisco today and ate a big meal on the plane. I think I would like to get acquainted with my little granddaughter, then go to bed."

As they started for the stairs, with Anna and the dogs running ahead of them and Kon trailing with the luggage, his mother said, "Anna is very much like Deema's sister, Nadia, used to be. Bright, inquisitive, full of life."

"Nadia died of a lung disease before her fourteenth birthday," Kon explained under his breath in English.

Meg's chest constricted. "And your father?"

"One day he went logging and his heart gave out. That was five years ago."

"How has she survived all these years alone?"

"Scrubbing floors and toilets in civic buildings."

"How old is she?"

"Sixty-five."

"She's wonderful, Kon."

"She is. So are you."

Much later that night, when the house had finally fallen quiet and the lights were turned off, Kon entered their bedroom, where Meg had been impatiently waiting for him.

"The last time I looked, Mama was reading the *Nutcracker* to Anna. She's actually picked up quite a few words from our bedtime stories."

"What could be more natural, my darling?" Meg whispered. She reached eagerly for him as he shrugged out of his robe and slid into the bed. "Mrs. Beezley told me she was exceptionally intelligent for her age. Mrs. Rosen said the same thing about her talent for the violin. She inherited those qualities from her father."

"And from her mother. She's also inherited the sweetness of her spirit from you," he murmured against her mouth, kissing her breathless. "When I left them, they were communicating with amazing facility."

Meg couldn't contain her emotions. "That book has been like a magical link between all of us, my darling."

He smoothed the hair from her forehead, staring into her very soul. "That's because the *Nutcracker* is magical. When Mama embraced me and started talking to me about the past, dozens of memories came flooding back. One of my strongest impressions was of her reading the *Nutcracker* to me when I was a child. That's why it made such an impact on me—and why I wanted you to have that particular book when you left Russia. It symbolized hope and love for me, Meggie. *Our* love. Now it has all come together in a living reality." His voice broke before he claimed her mouth once more and drew her fully into his arms.

"I've yearned for you, Meggie. I love you with such a terrible hunger it frightens me."

"I'm frightened to think I almost lost you again."

"I won't lie to you, Meggie. After I left the house at Christmas, I'd pretty well lost hope for us. But I had to try again."

"Thank God you did! I love you so much! Kon—" She gasped in ecstasy at the first touch of his hand against her flesh. The pleasure was almost unbearable. "I can't believe this is happening. Am I dreaming?"

"Does it matter?" he asked in a husky voice. "We're together at last. Any more questions or explanations will have to wait, because nothing else is—or ever will be—as important as you here with me.

"Love me, Meggie," he begged, the pain of longing in his voice and body echoing hers. She gave herself up to the only man who would ever be all things to her—guardian, friend, lover, husband, father of her children.

Not many other women had traveled so far from home, on so strange and precarious a path to their ultimate destiny and fulfillment.

But she'd do it again for the love of one Konstantin Rudenko, the prince of her heart and, most assuredly, of Anna's.

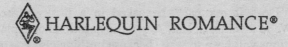

HARLEQUIN ROMANCE®

brings you

More Romances Celebrating Love, Families and Children!

We promised in December, after bringing you
The Nutcracker Prince and **The Santa Sleuth**,
that we would have more wonderful titles in our
KIDS & KISSES series. True to our promise, in January
we have the wonderfully warm story **No Ties**
(Harlequin Romance #3344) by Rosemary Gibson. When
Cassie goes to work for Professor Adam Merrick, she finds
not only love and marriage, but a ready-made family!

Watch for more of these special romances from favorite
Harlequin Romance authors in the coming months:

February	#3347	A Valentine for Daisy	Betty Neels
March	#3351	Leonie's Luck	Emma Goldrick
April	#3357	The Baby Business	Rebecca Winters
May	#3359	Bachelor's Family	Jessica Steele

Available wherever Harlequin books are sold.

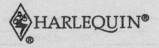

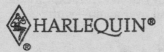

The proprietors of Weddings, Inc. hope you
have enjoyed visiting Eternity, Massachusetts.
And if you missed any of the exciting Weddings,
Inc. titles, here is your opportunity to complete
your collection:

Harlequin Superromance	#598	*Wedding Invitation* by Marisa Carroll	$3.50 U.S. ☐ $3.99 CAN. ☐
Harlequin Romance	#3319	*Expectations* by Shannon Waverly	$2.99 U.S. ☐ $3.50 CAN. ☐
Harlequin Temptation	#502	*Wedding Song* by Vicki Lewis Thompson	$2.99 U.S. ☐ $3.50 CAN. ☐
Harlequin American Romance	#549	*The Wedding Gamble* by Muriel Jensen	$3.50 U.S. ☐ $3.99 CAN. ☐
Harlequin Presents	#1692	*The Vengeful Groom* by Sara Wood	$2.99 U.S. ☐ $3.50 CAN. ☐
Harlequin Intrigue	#298	*Edge of Eternity* by Jasmine Cresswell	$2.99 U.S. ☐ $3.50 CAN. ☐
Harlequin Historical	#248	*Vows* by Margaret Moore	$3.99 U.S. ☐ $4.50 CAN. ☐

HARLEQUIN BOOKS...
NOT THE SAME OLD STORY

TOTAL AMOUNT	$
POSTAGE & HANDLING	$
($1.00 for one book, 50¢ for each additional)	
APPLICABLE TAXES*	$ _____
TOTAL PAYABLE	$ _____
(check or money order—please do not send cash)	

To order, complete this form and send it, along with a check or money order for the
total above, payable to Harlequin Books, to: **In the U.S.:** 3010 Walden Avenue,
P.O. Box 9047, Buffalo, NY 14269-9047; **In Canada:** P.O. Box 613, Fort Erie, Ontario,
L2A 5X3.

Name: _____

Address: _____ City: _____

State/Prov.: _____ Zip/Postal Code: _____

*New York residents remit applicable sales taxes.
Canadian residents remit applicable GST and provincial taxes.

WED-F

This holiday, join four hunky heroes under the mistletoe for

Christmas Kisses

Cuddle under a fluffy quilt, with a cup of hot chocolate and these romances sure to warm you up:

#561 HE'S A REBEL (also a Studs title)
Linda Randall Wisdom

#562 THE BABY AND THE BODYGUARD
Jule McBride

#563 THE GIFT-WRAPPED GROOM
M.J. Rodgers

#564 A TIMELESS CHRISTMAS
Pat Chandler

Celebrate the season with all four holiday books sealed with a Christmas kiss—coming to you in December, only from Harlequin American Romance!

CHRISTMAS STALKINGS

All wrapped up in spine-tingling packages, here are three books guaranteed to chill your spine...and warm your hearts this holiday season!

#302 THE KID WHO STOLE CHRISTMAS
Linda Stevens

#303 I'LL BE HOME FOR CHRISTMAS
Dawn Stewardson

#304 BEARING GIFTS
Aimée Thurlo

This December, fill your stockings with the "Christmas Stalkings"—for the best in romantic suspense. Only from

HARLEQUIN®

I N T R I G U E®